Is

Is

Derek Webb

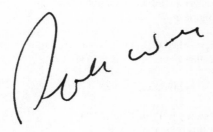

WWW.TROLLCARNIVAL.CO.UK

Troll Carnival
The Old Surgery
Napier Street
Cardigan
SA43 1ED
www.trollcarnival.co.uk

First published in 2010
© Derek Webb

Edited by Penny Thomas

ISBN: 978-1-906998-11-0

Published with the financial support of
the Welsh Books Council.

Photograph of Isambard Kingdom Brunel in front of the
chains of the Great Eastern by kind permission of the
Institution of Civil Engineers

Design: www.theundercard.co.uk
Typesetting: www.lucyllew.com

Printed & bound by Gwasg Gomer, Llandysul

British Library Cataloguing in Publication Data
A catalogue record of this book is available
from the British Library

Find out more about
Is and Brunel at
www.ikbrunel.org.uk

For Briony with much love and thanks
for her inspiration, enthusiasm
and encouragement.

Contents

Is

1
This is Is

It was during my second year of secondary school that I first met Is. Mr Gregory, our form master, swept into our classroom like a great black bat one morning with Is in tow. We didn't see her at first because she was so tiny, even though she was twelve. Or maybe she was cowering behind Mr Gregory, who really could look very frightening with his black cape on. All the masters at our school wore these capes. Not many teachers do now of course, but this was in 1972 and things were very different then.

'Good morning, boys and girls,' Mr Gregory wheezed and his lips drew back as he spoke, exposing his horrible yellowing teeth.

None of us in Class 2F knew why Mr Gregory didn't go and see a dentist with his teeth. Maybe he couldn't find one brave enough to peer into his mouth. I certainly wouldn't have liked to be a dentist coming face to face with Mr Gregory's molars, I can tell you.

Nevertheless, we all chanted back at him in unison: 'Good morning, Mr Gregory!'

'I bring you a new girl!' exclaimed Mr Gregory, as if he was bringing a sacrifice to some ancient ritual. Which, come to think of it, he was.

Is scurried forward like a rabbit, her tiny eyes darting everywhere before her. She looked so pathetic and wimpish that most of us couldn't help giggling at the sight of her, until old Gregory yelled out 'Quiet!'

'I will not have this behaviour in my class!' he bellowed, and the vein on his neck grew bigger and redder and even more disgusting than usual.

Mr Gregory on a bad day was enough to send shivers through the toughest nuts in the whole of St Leonards School – even oiks like Wilkins up in the sixth form knew not to cross him.

For the newcomer to our class, standing there feebly in front of this great bull of a man, it must have been a truly terrifying experience. Mr Gregory had by now mounted the podium on which his desk was perched and he lifted his great carcass on to the top of the desk and sat there with one foot on the floor and the other dangling loose.

'This is Isabel Williams,' Mr Gregory continued, indicating Is with his foot. 'She is joining us today and I want you all to make her welcome. Understood?'

'Yes, Mr Gregory,' we all muttered with varying degrees of enthusiasm.

'Good! Right, Isabel, you can go and sit yourself down at that empty desk next to Robert Morgan there.' And he actually nudged Isabel towards me with the tip of his shoe.

She sat down quietly and Mr Gregory went through the morning's ritual of doing the register with everyone calling out 'Here, Sir' as their name was read out.

When he got to 'Williams', there was no answer and Mr Gregory repeated her name more loudly. Still she didn't respond, and this time Mr Gregory accompanied his shout of 'Isabel Williams' with the thwack of a metal ruler on the desk. Isabel jumped at this and answered in a small, trembling voice.

'Here, Sir.'

'I am so glad you're awake, Isabel,' replied Mr Gregory sarcastically. He ticked the register and then continued to the last boy.

'Wilson.'

'Here, Sir!'

'Good!' The book was slammed shut and pushed across the desk and we all filed out to the school hall for assembly.

We weren't allowed to talk in class of course. So it wasn't until lunchtime that I first spoke to Isabel. Most of the kids in my class had school dinners, but because I lived so close to the school, I used to go home instead. I was setting off as usual across the playground when I saw her on her own by the school gate. I don't often talk to girls, not even the ones in my class, but Is looked so miserable and was sort of staring at me, so I felt I had to do something.

'Hello,' I said gruffly, 'why aren't you with the others? They'll all be stuffing their faces by now!'

She just looked up at me and said nothing, then I realised that she obviously didn't know where to go.

'Hasn't anyone bothered to show you where they serve lunch. What a load of ignoramuses!'

'No, it's not that,' she replied. 'I'm not hungry.'

'Not hungry?'

'Well, to tell you the truth I haven't brought any money for school dinners. No one said anything about it.'

'But didn't your parents give you any money?' I asked, astonished.

'No.'

'But that's silly. You've got to eat something.' I sounded like my mother. 'Haven't you got any money at all?'

'No.'

'And didn't anybody ask your mother when she brought you along this morning?'

'I came on my own.'

'You don't live far then?' I said, relieved that she'd be able to go home for lunch.

'Walton Road.'

'Walton Road? But that's miles! You got the school bus did you?'

'No.'

'Bike?'

'No.'

'Don't tell me you walked.'

'Yes.'

I stared at her for a few seconds, amazed that her parents would let her walk all that way to school and not even give her money for a school lunch. Then I looked at the new watch I'd got for my birthday.

'Oh no, is that the time? My mum'll kill me! I'll see you later, okay?'

'Okay,' she replied and I set off down the tarmac path towards the road. But something was bothering me. I hadn't quite got to the end when I had a thought.

'You can come back with me if you like. I only live two roads away. I'm sure my mum will find you something to eat.'

For the first time I saw her smile. Her face lit up at the idea. But the smile faded just as quickly as a question crossed her mind.

'Are you sure?'

'Course.'

'She won't mind?'

'Nah, don't be daft. Come on!'

We were over ten minutes late by the time we got back to my house and Mum was not in the best of moods.

'And what time do you call...' she started to say and then realised that I wasn't on my own.

'Sorry we're late,' I said in my best, most apologetic voice.

'So I should think. Aren't you going to introduce me to your friend then?'

'Sorry,' I said again, 'this is Isabel.'

'Is.'

'Sorry? Is what, dear?' said my mother.

'My name's Isabel,' she explained. 'But my friends call me Is.'

'This is Is. Is is her name!' I said laughing. And then I knew I would be very good friends with her.

'Oh it is, is it?' replied my mother, joining in

the joke at last. 'And I suppose you'd like some of Robert's lunch would you, Is?'

'Oh, no; not at all, Mrs Morgan. I'm not in the slightest bit hungry, really.'

'Yes she is, Mum,' I said. 'Are there some extra chips or something that – er – Is could have?'

Mum smiled. 'Oh, I expect so. Just sit yourselves down at the table while I have a look,' she said and went off into the kitchen.

'Your mum's really nice,' whispered Is as we pulled out the chairs.

'Nice? Mum?' I'd never really considered the possibility before, but I supposed she was right. 'She's okay,' I answered with a shrug.

'I wish mine was like her.'

'What's your mum like then?' I asked.

'It's my stepmother,' Is replied and then she lowered her voice until I could barely hear her. 'And she's a cow.'

The way she said it, with such feeling, I remember actually being shocked.

'Oh,' was all I could answer.

'My real mum died soon after I was born,' she explained. 'And my dad got remarried when I was four. Probably couldn't cope on his own.'

'S'pose not.'

But then we were interrupted by my mum

reappearing with two plates of beefburgers and chips.

'Here we are,' she said. 'Get this down you.'

She set the plates down in front of us and then suddenly realised something.

'Oh, I am sorry Is, I clean forgot to ask... you do like beefburgers, don't you? You're not vegetarian or anything?'

'Yes thanks, Mrs Morgan, they're my favourite.'

'Oh, good!' She breathed a sign of relief. 'I'm so glad and these are ones I made myself too. They're not like your shop-bought ones. Much nicer.'

'Where do they come from then, Mum?' I asked.

'Well, originally from a cow of course,' she answered, with a smile on her face. But she didn't expect the reaction she got from the two of us. Is and I had both collapsed in a fit of giggles at the mere mention of 'cow'.

'Well, I didn't think it was quite that funny!' said my mum, perplexed.

'It wasn't, Mrs Morgan...' Isabel started saying without thinking.

'Pardon?' said my mother with a touch of annoyance in her voice.

'Oh, I didn't mean it wasn't funny,' explained Isabel, keen to correct any misunderstanding. 'I mean it was funny, but not in the way you meant it. Do you see?'

'I'm afraid I don't. Anyway you two, get on and eat up or you'll be late back to school.'

* * *

After that it began to be a bit of a habit for Is to come back and have lunch at my place. She came round a couple of times a week at least. The other days she used to have sandwiches, but I don't remember her once eating school dinners. No wonder she was so terribly small.

Looking back on it, it was a terrible cheek really. Not that Mum minded. Well, not too much I don't think. Although she did mention it once in a roundabout sort of way.

'Does Isabel not have any other friends then, Robert?' she asked me out of the blue one evening, as she looked up from the magazine she was reading.

'I don't know. Why?' I asked in return. Then I thought a bit more and added 'She goes around with Ronnie – you know, Veronica Biggleswade – and sometimes I see her after school with Susan Timson. But not that many, no.'

'I didn't think so,' was all Mum said to that and went straight back to her magazine.

That got me thinking. It was true that Is didn't hang around with hardly any of the other kids in our class, except me. She always seemed to keep herself to herself. Nothing wrong with that of course. But it did mean that the school bullies couldn't resist talking the mickey out of her.

'What's up, Isabel,' someone like Kevin Ryder would say if they caught her standing on her own in a corner of the playground. 'Don't no one wanna come near you then? Got BO have you? Smell do you? Bit of a stinker are you, eh? Don't you wash then? Eh? Eh?'

And then he would go around the playground yelling out 'Isabel's got smelly armpits'. Or something equally offensive.

Some people just don't have any brains.

It didn't seem to bother Isabel though. Most of the time she just ignored them and that's usually the best thing to do, of course. People got fed up with teasing her and it having no effect. In the end they gave up. After all, there's no point in calling someone names if they don't seem to care. Where's the fun in that?

I admired her for that. She never seemed to lose her temper and rarely even answered back. So, when she did, it was all the more surprising. Especially as it wasn't a brainless idiot like Kevin that she lost her temper with, but with Mr Phillips, our Physics teacher.

2
An Arch Rival

The school we were at was called a grammar school and I suppose we were very lucky to be there, although we certainly didn't think so at the time. Many of our friends had gone to the local comprehensive school instead. Back then comprehensives were quite a new idea and there were lots of people saying they were a rotten idea and just as many saying they were great. Frankly I couldn't care less either way. I mean, school's school isn't it? Whatever you call it. And I certainly didn't see being at my school as a good thing. It could be very boring.

It was on a Wednesday morning that we did Physics. We all trooped in and sat at our usual desks. Is was given a desk across the aisle from me, near the front of the class.

Mr Phillips started the lesson by going through a lot of the usual boring stuff and finding out what we'd remembered from last term, which wasn't much.

The one thing I remembered was how light is reflected when it strikes a highly polished surface. Since last term they'd put in some new spotlights at the front of the classroom. The funny thing was that Mr Phillips had a really bald head and one of these spotlights was aimed right at it.

Talk about dazzling!

Poor old Mr Phillips. He wasn't that old really either, well not that old. He'd just lost his hair early – probably having to deal with the 'likes of us' as he put it. Anyway, today, how light behaves obviously wasn't the subject of his lesson.

'Right,' he started, 'for today's exercise, I want you all to imagine you're building a bridge over a river. Now it's a very wide river, so you'll need to take that into account.'

Trevor Smart's hand shot up.

'How wide exactly, Sir?'

'Oh, I don't know, Trevor. Let's say 130 feet.' In those days, of course, we still used to measure everything in yards, feet and inches.

Trevor's hand shot up again. 'Is it a very deep river, Sir?'

Trevor Smart was, not surprisingly, known as 'Clever Trevor' because he was always sticking his hand up and asking the stupidest questions.

'It's deep enough, Trevor, okay?'

'What's the ground like either side of the river, Sir? Is it rock or clay or what?'

I turned and was amazed to find that it wasn't Clever Trevor asking the question this time, it was Is.

'Does it really matter, Isabel?' asked Mr Phillips with a frown on his face.

'Well, yes, it's really very important, Sir,' replied Is.

'It's rock, all right. The bridge is 130 feet wide and the ground either side is rock. Satisfied?'

'Yes, thank you, Sir.'

'Good, well if we can all get on... as I was saying, for today's exercise, I'd like you to draw a bridge. It can be any kind of bridge you like. But it has to be strong enough to support a road that carries a lot of heavy traffic, okay?'

Mr Phillips looked around the classroom for response. He got none.

Undaunted he carried on. 'There are basically four types of bridge. Now I won't expect you to know all of them.' Just as well. 'But hopefully you will come up with a couple of different types amongst you.'

Miracles might happen, his voice seemed to say.

'Anyway,' he continued, 'what you need to think about is how you are going to support the weight on the bridge and what is going to prevent it from falling down. Is that clear?'

He looked around the classroom at a sea of what seemed to be staring, blank faces.

'Oh, good grief,' he muttered as he picked up a chalk.

In those days, schools didn't have white-boards, but large blackboards which teachers wrote on with chalk. You still see them behind the whiteboards in some schools. (Confusingly, these 'blackboards' were often green!) There were usually two of them which slid up and down on runners, one behind the other, so you could write on one and then pull the other down to carry on, which is what Mr Phillips did.

'Look and pay attention any of you who aren't clear,' he said. 'If this is a lorry...'

He drew a box shape on the board and then drew two circles under it.

'And this is the road it's sitting on...' he drew a line below the box shape. 'And this is the river...' he drew some wiggly lines underneath. 'Then how are you going to support the road and the lorry?'

'With a bridge, Sir!' yelled out Clever Trev, all excited.

'Of course, with a bridge, boy!' screamed back Mr Phillips. 'That is what I am asking you to draw!'

Mr Phillips took a deep breath. Then he sat down and pushed his glasses up on top of his shiny bald head.

A few seconds later he let out a deep sigh.

Then he pulled the glasses back down again and peered through them with his piggy eyes.

Finally he clasped his hands together in front of him, like he was praying, before speaking again.

'Let me give you a bit of help shall I?' He smiled a sickly smile around the room and we all looked away when it was pointing in our direction. 'Just think of some of the bridges you know...'

'I don't know no bridges,' said Steven Clarke with a sullen look on his face.

'You don't know any bridges,' replied Mr Phillips. 'Not you don't know no bridges.'

'I know, that's what I said,' answered Steven, failing to get the point.

Mr Phillips sighed and carried on. 'I'm sure you all know some bridges, even young Clarke here. How many of you have been to London, for example?'

Since we were only about twenty-five miles

from London, everyone put their hands up, including Steven

'Ri   ued Mr Phillips. 'Now
we're   So think about all the
bridges   s the Thames. Battersea
Bridge,   Hammersmith Bridge,
Putney   Bridge even. Try and
rememb   draw that if you like.'

After   ed at us all, as if daring
us to ask   s. No one did.

'Right,' he announced. 'Ten minutes. Then we'll have a look at what you've drawn and those that look promising we'll make into models to see if they work. Okay, get on with it.'

For a full minute I stared at the blank sheet of paper in front of me. What on earth was I going to draw, I wondered?

I tried to think of some of the bridges in London that I'd been across but couldn't remember anything about them really. After all, a bridge is a bridge, isn't it?

Trevor Smart seemed to have no such problem. He was scribbling away furiously with his pencil. Only occasionally did he stop to scratch his head before pressing on with his grand design.

Oh well, I thought, it's time I did something myself. Mr Phillips had got down from his desk and had started to wander up and down the rows of desks, peering over our shoulders at our handiwork. I couldn't let him see that I had done nothing at all.

I drew the lorry as he had done. Then I drew the road underneath it. Next I drew in the wiggly lines to represent the river and did the banks. All I needed was the bridge itself.

In desperation I lightly drew in three round arches underneath the road. I had seen a bridge like that somewhere near my grandmother's house, I remembered. And, surprisingly, it looked all right. Yes, it actually looked like a bridge! So it was that easy after all!

I thickened up the lines and then, feeling pleased with myself, I glanced across at Is to see how she was getting on. Unlike Trev, she was drawing very slowly and was bent over her paper covering it with her arm.

'Right, just a couple more minutes then we'll have a look at what you've got,' announced Mr Phillips.

There was a flurry of activity, with everyone drawing frantically. Even Kevin Ryder managed to hold his pencil the right way up.

But needless to say it was Trevor Smart who finished first. He put down his pencil and turned over his sheet of paper with a great flourish.

As if that wasn't enough, he sat back in his chair, folded his arms and looked around the room at the rest of us with a stupid grin on his face. 'Look at me,' his smile seemed to say, 'aren't I clever?'

It got right up my nose, I can tell you. So I did what you would expect me to do – I stuck my tongue out at him.

Unluckily for me, my tongue went out at exactly the moment that Mr Phillips turned round to come up between the row of desks I was sitting in and the one Trevor was in.

'Morgan! How dare you stick your tongue out at me like that?'

'I wasn't, Sir,' I protested.

'Don't lie to me, boy, I saw you!' yelled Mr Phillips.

'But it wasn't you I was sticking my tongue out at, Sir.'

'If it wasn't me, who was it?'

'Trevor, Sir.'

'Trevor?'

'Yes, Sir.' The second the words left my mouth, I knew it was completely the wrong thing to say. But then, whatever I said would have been wrong I suppose.

'Stand up, Morgan,' Mr Phillips instructed and I shuffled to my feet. 'Are you in the habit of sticking your tongue out at your fellow pupils?'

I had never thought of Trevor as a 'fellow pupil' before, but I didn't say that. Instead I meekly replied 'No'.

'No, what?' screamed Mr Phillips back at me.

'No, Sir.'

'Then make sure it does not happen again, Morgan. Clear?'

'Yes, Sir,' I said, amazed that I had got off so lightly.

My guess was that Mr Phillips detested Trevor as much as the rest of us did and, secretly, would have liked to have stuck his tongue out at him too.

But of course he didn't. Instead he clapped his hands together and yelled out, 'Right, time's up!'

'Aw, Sir...' some of the class protested; they hadn't yet finished. Still it was their own fault. They should have been getting on with their bridge drawings instead of listening to Mr Phillips having a go at me.

'No, I'm sorry, that's it,' said Mr Phillips. 'Ten minutes is what I said.

'Okay then, let's see what you've got....' He looked round the room as he wondered who to pick on first and all the while he was sucking his lips noisily. He did this whenever he was thinking – it sounded disgusting.

Anyway I was pleased to see where his gaze came to rest.

'Ah, Trevor!' said Mr Phillips, 'Let us all share your view of what this bridge should look like. Hold up your drawing so we can all see, will you?'

Trevor slowly turned over the sheet of drawing paper and, holding it carefully by two corners, he lifted it up. Much as I hate Trevor, I had to admit it wasn't bad. Well, actually, it was very good. Even Mr Phillips was impressed, I could tell.

'And what sort of bridge have you drawn there, Trevor?' he asked.

'It's a suspension bridge, Sir,' replied Trev and his smarmy smile returned.

'Yes, that is correct, Trevor. And could you explain to the class how it works?'

So then Trev launched into this great load of waffle about the bridge being suspended by cables or something. I couldn't really understand a word of what he was saying. It sounded amazingly elaborate, I know that.

Mr Phillips seemed to understand though. His head was going up and down like one of those disgusting nodding dogs you see in the back windows of cars. And the more Clever Trev prattled on, the more Mr Phillips nodded. It was enough to make me want to throw up.

Nobody else had drawn anything as complicated as Trev's bridge. Susan Timson had simply made the road much fatter and said it was a big girder. I didn't think she'd get away with that, but Mr Phillips said it was all right – it was one of the types of bridges he was looking for.

Mine, as it turned out, was one of the other types. I couldn't believe my luck when I held up my drawing and Mr Phillips said, 'Well done, Robert! That's an arch bridge you've drawn there. Perhaps you'd like to explain the principle behind it.'

What did I know about the principle behind it?

'Well,' I started, unsure of what I had actually done, 'the road here is just supported by these three arches under it, that's all.'

'That's it exactly!'

I couldn't believe it. I'd actually done something right for a change.

'An arch, you see,' continued Mr Phillips, 'is a very strong structure indeed. Provided that the shape is right it will support an enormous amount of weight. Your arches are very nearly semi-circular so the force acting downwards spreads itself smoothly over the top of the arch and down each side.'

'Spreads itself smoothly...?' What was he on about now, I thought – it sounded more like peanut butter than bridges. Of course, I didn't admit I didn't understand. Not a bit of it. I simply held the drawing up higher to make sure that everyone in the class had a good view – and would be able to recognise a really classy arch bridge in the future when they saw one.

But Mr Phillips hadn't finished yet.

'And, wisely, I see you have chosen to use three arches because of the span. The river is – how wide did I say it was? 130 feet – ah, yes. Very well done, Robert.'

But, instead of sitting back down again, I was so flushed with my success that I continued holding my drawing up.

'I said "thank you, Robert". You may put your drawing down now.'

At that I dropped it on the desk, but it floated on to the floor and I had to scurry around under Trevor Smart's chair to retrieve it. When I got it back there was a dirty footprint from one of Trevor's size 6s on it. I'd see to him later...

But none of this prevented Mr Phillips from wittering on.

'So now we have a suspension bridge, a girder bridge and an arch bridge,' he said. 'I wonder if any of you have drawn another sort of bridge...' he paused for a minute then turned to Is. 'Isabel, let's see your bridge, shall we?'

Isabel lifted her drawing up so we could all see.

Mr Phillips stared at it then clucked his tongue, sounding like an old hen.

'Oh, dear me, Isabel, no,' he chided. 'You've missed the point entirely, haven't you?'

'What do you mean, Sir?' asked Isabel in a hurt voice.

'Well look at it, Isabel. What do you call this?'

'It's an arch bridge, Sir, like Robert's.'

'But it wouldn't work, would it, Isabel. You've only drawn one arch across all that width. Why, it's almost flat in the middle!'

'Of course it would work, Sir!' I couldn't believe it was Isabel speaking.

'What did you say, Isabel?' Mr Phillips, I could tell, was already bristling.

'I said of course it would work – Sir!' replied Isabel.

'And what do you propose that this – "bridge" of yours would be made from?'

'Bricks.'

'Bricks? Hah!' Mr Phillips scoffed.

Even I could see that it wouldn't work. My own effort was much better considering. At least mine had enough arches to support the lorry, which was more than hers did. Arguing with Mr Phillips was pretty dumb too. But she wasn't about to give in.

'Yes, bricks!' she yelled defiantly and stood up with her eyes blazing.

I'd never seen Is like that before. It was a quite extraordinary scene. Mr Phillips, needless to say, was not amused.

'How dare you talk to me like that, my girl? How dare you answer back? I will not have it, do you hear? I will not have it! Your bridge would fall down. It couldn't possibly support its own weight, let alone the lorry's. And that is that!'

I thought Isabel would burst out crying there and then. But, amazingly, she didn't. She just spoke very quietly.

'You are quite wrong, Sir. You might think that it wouldn't even support its own weight, but you would be quite wrong, Sir. As long as the arching forces are properly calculated and evenly trans-mitted, it would work. The design is perfect. You, Sir, do not know what you are talking about.'

'Get to the Head! GET TO THE HEAD! This instant. This very instant, Isabel. How dare you... how dare you?'

Mr Phillips was spluttering so much that dribble was running down his chin. I'd never seen Mr Phillips in such a terrible rage before. The whole class went pale.

Is didn't show any signs of trembling or

anything. She just put her drawing carefully down on the desk. Then she glanced at me, turned and walked slowly out of the room, down to the Head's office.

She got two nights' detention for her trouble. Still, it could have been worse. I did feel sorry for her, even though it was her own fault really.

Mind you, it made her a lot more popular with the rest of the class, standing up to Mr Phillips like that. Even Kevin Ryder grudgingly admitted she was all right.

'For a girl,' he added.

3
River Walk

Luckily we didn't have any more lessons with Mr Phillips that week or who knows what would have happened. And by the following week I reckoned he would have cooled down a bit.

The rest of the week passed pretty much without incident, although Clever Trev got his comeuppance for stamping on my drawing. Somehow a bottle of ink leaked all over his English homework. I can't imagine how it could have happened...

The weekend came and I was planning to do no more than laze around. As it was, Brian, a friend who lived down the road, came round on Saturday morning with a new plane he'd made and we went over to the playing fields and got it going.

It was very good. He'd made it out of a balsa wood kit but it had a real engine and it went really well. Brian was all right. I liked him a lot. But I didn't see that much of him because he went to St Luke's, which was the local comprehensive school.

We used to go to the same school but then I went on to the grammar school instead. I don't know why really, in many ways Brian was a lot cleverer than me. I certainly couldn't make a plane like he had. I'd be all fingers and thumbs. I was quite good at lazing in front of the television though, which was what I did on Saturday evening.

I remember there was a programme called Opportunity Knocks, which was a bit like Britain's Got Talent, and my favourite, Doctor Who, which by then was on its third Doctor. I think the Doctor was fighting some aliens called the Sea Devils who lived in an abandoned sea fort or something. And the great thing was I was able to see it in colour, which was pretty cool back then. Lots of people I knew still had black and white televisions, even though colour TV had been around for about five years.

Next day I got up about ten, got myself some Weetabix and plonked myself down on the enormous cushion we had on the floor in the sitting room.

That's when Mum came in with her oh-so-healthy suggestion.

'How about a walk?' she asked.

I said nothing, and pretended I hadn't heard,

hoping the idea would soon be forgotten. Dad was slumped on the sofa reading the Sunday paper and he was usually about as keen on going for walks as I was. But you never can tell with parents. Just when I expected him to say 'not today, Jean, if you don't mind' or something like that, what do you suppose he goes and says?

'What a great idea, Jean! Lovely spring morning like this. Ideal.' And he pushed the paper aside and stood up.

I couldn't believe it.

'Oh, do we have to, Mum?' I tried.

'Yes, come on Rob, it'll do you good.'

'Oh, Mum,' I pleaded, but I knew I was on to a loser.

'I know,' piped up Dad, 'what about a walk along the river.'

That settled it. Ten minutes later we were in the car and on our way down to the river by Maidenhead. We parked the car and walked down an overgrown track, eventually getting on to a footpath that ran between some hedges and down towards the Thames.

Even at this point the river is quite wide, and on the opposite bank, there were really large houses with boats moored alongside. Some of them even had their own private boathouses.

As we came level with the river a sleek white catamaran boat sailed past us, churning up the water as it went. In the other direction, a bright blue canoe slipped by with its two canoeists – dressed in clashing red – paddling away furiously.

From somewhere behind me came the sound of someone sawing logs with a chain-saw, which nearly drowned the quacks of a dozen or more ducks as they swam rapidly towards a small island in the middle of the river.

Then the path dived in between high hedges, cutting out our view of the river. On our right there were fields that we could just glimpse through the hedge. Reluctantly I had to agree it was a good day for a walk. For the time of year it was brilliant. The sky overhead was completely blue and the sun shone down brightly, but it wasn't hot, just right, with a nice light breeze.

The hedges finished and we came out by some large houses on our side of the river. Their back gardens appeared to run right down to the water's edge where many of them had boats moored. For a minute it looked like we were actually about to go right through their gardens, but we were obviously still on the path.

If these houses were large, they were nothing compared to the ones on the other bank. There was a huge black and white, Tudor-looking monstrosity which had an enormous turret. And it didn't just have a landing stage for a boat either. It had its own small private dock!

People around here must be incredibly rich, I thought.

And, while I was still thinking about that, I caught sight of something far, far more astonishing.

Through the trees ahead was a bridge that looked horribly familiar. I stopped and puzzled over it for a second and then it came to me. It was Is's bridge!

It was pretty well exactly as she'd drawn it. At least that's what it looked like. It had the same low sweep, the same lines as she'd painstakingly drawn three days ago in Mr Phillips' class.

There it was: the same impossibly flat arch she had in her drawing. Except there wasn't just one arch but two, spanning the river and meeting at a little island midway.

As I stared at it amazed, a train thundered across, which made me realise how large the bridge actually was. One thing was certain, this was Isabel's bridge all right; the one that Mr Phillips had said was ridiculous!

Then it disappeared from view behind some trees again so I decided to run on to have a closer look.

'Hey, where are you going?' asked Mum. 'We're not going much further, you know.'

'I must see this bridge first,' I said, without thinking how daft that sounded.

I ran on, ignoring their protests. I couldn't believe it. The drawing that Is had done had been very detailed, unlike my scrappy affair. Looking at the bridge, which was getting bigger and bigger by the step, it was hard to believe that Is hadn't copied hers from a photograph. It was just the same in every respect.

Beyond it I could see another bridge, a road bridge, and this was much more like the one I'd drawn. It had lots of arches: there must have been four or five of them, to span the same width of river. But this one leapt across in just two broad arches.

It did look impossible; it did look like Mr Phillips said. It was difficult to see how it could ever stay up. The centre section was virtually flat. But stay up it undoubtedly had for a great many years. This bridge was a hundred years old if it was a day.

I was nearly up to it now. A motor boat chugged underneath it, completely dwarfed by the bridge's size.

'Come back, Robert, will you?' called my mother from some distance behind.

'Rob, do as your mother says,' joined in Dad.

'Won't be a second,' I yelled back over my shoulder. 'There's something I want to look at.'

The path continued underneath one of the arches and I walked through to the other side. As I did, I looked up at the bricks, many of which were stained white from lime or something.

Light reflected from the river created patterns on the underside of the bridge and I stopped and stared up; transfixed by the great spans of bricks, millions and millions of bricks.

I actually thought it rather beautiful. It was… what's the word? Elegant. Elegant's not a word I'd usually use. Never do. But it is exactly the word to describe that bridge.

Once I'd walked through to the other side I could see the other bridge clearly. There were indeed about five arches to carry the road. A much more typical bridge all round.

'Robert! Are you coming or not?' I was jolted out of my thoughts by my father.

'Sorry, just coming,' I said automatically and turned back towards my parents, every now and then shooting a glance over my shoulder at my discovery.

'Have you seen that bridge?' I panted as I got back to where they were waiting. 'Isn't it great?'

'It's quite famous,' said my dad, matter-of-factly, 'It's Brunel's.'

'Brunel's?'

'He built it. You've heard of Brunel haven't you?'

'Well, I think so,' I said, not too sure whether I had or not.

'He was a famous Victorian engineer,' continued my father. 'He built the Great Western Railway. You've heard of that I assume?'

'That's the railway that goes over that bridge is it?'

'It starts in Paddington,' said Dad.

I brightened. 'Oh, yes, I've been there!'

'And it goes all the way down to South Wales and the West Country.'

'Oh, right,' I muttered, not really interested. 'So this bridge, it's famous you say?'

'Oh, yes.'

* * *

I couldn't wait to get back to school on the Monday.

'Whatever's up with you, Robert?' asked my mother as I appeared in the kitchen at half past seven. 'Have you any idea what time it is?'

'Half past seven,' I replied. 'Can I help myself to some Weetabix?'

'Yes, here, I'll get it for you,' she said, reaching

up into the wall cupboard above her head. 'But that's not what I meant. What I mean is, what are you doing up so early?'

'Going to school,' I said, stating the obvious. 'I'm really looking forward to it.'

'Well, I must say this is a great change. And, if I don't have to spend so long in the morning trying to wake you up in future, I won't know what to do with my time!'

'Oh, there's no need to start worrying about that, Mum,' I replied cheerfully. 'I won't be making a habit of it. It's only for this morning!'

'Thought it was too good to be true,' she sighed. 'Go on, get your Weetabix.'

I bolted it down, grabbed my things and tore off up the road. But despite me being so early, I was amazed to find Isabel already in the playground when I got to school.

'What's up?' I said cheerfully. 'Couldn't you sleep either?'

'Dad and Penny had a bust up.'

'Who's Penny?'

'My stepmum.'

'Oh, I see,' I paused. 'Serious?'

'She screamed at him to get out. Told him she never wanted to see him again. Then he went out, slamming the door behind him. But, just before he did, he took this little porcelain statue of a ballerina from the table in the hall and threw it on to the floor. It was her very favourite thing and it lay there in a million bits. She went completely mad.'

'When was this?' I whispered. I felt more concerned because Is wasn't whimpering or any-thing. She was just quietly relating the facts as if she had been watching something that didn't really concern her.

'About six-thirty this morning.'

'So what did you do?'

'Got dressed and came to school of course. What else was there to do?'

'You've been here all this time.'

'Yes.'

I was amazed.

'What have you been doing?'

'Just thinking.'

'Oh.' I didn't know what else to say.

Isabel looked at me in an old-fashioned sort of way and then smiled. 'What about you? Why are you here so early? You look very cheerful for a Monday morning.'

'You'll never guess,' I started.

'Try me.'

'I saw your bridge.'

'What bridge?'

'You know; the one you drew.'

'Oh, that bridge.'

I was really disappointed. She didn't seem in the slightest bit interested. But then, her parents had just had a blazing row, and even if she gave the impression of not being concerned, it must have had an effect on her.

But I persisted anyway, I was sure she'd be pleased.

'Yes that bridge, Isabel. The bridge you drew in Mr Phillips' class, the one you got into trouble over...'

'What about it?'

'Well, I've only been and seen it, haven't I?' I said proudly. 'It's at Maidenhead. It's a railway bridge. And it's exactly like you drew it, you know with those really flat arches that look impossible and all that...'

She looked puzzled.

'Yes, I know.'

I was flabbergasted.

'What do you mean, "you know"? Are you saying you've seen it before?'

'Yes, of course.'

'Then why didn't you say something to old Phillips when he was going on about it? He was wrong. Your bridge could have been built. It has been built. It's there. I've seen it.'

'What's the point?'

'My dad says it's famous. So old Phillips should have known about it anyway, shouldn't he? Even less reason for behaving like he did.'

'What's it matter? There were lots of people like Mr Phillips when it was built. They thought it'd fall down too. Some of them even wanted it to. I didn't care then and I don't care now.'

'What do you mean? I don't follow you.'

'Nothing.'

She turned away and starting kicking at a loose bit of gravel in the playground, ignoring me.

I was starting to feel a bit angry with her by now. She'd argued with a teacher, and ended up with detention when all she had to say was that it was a real bridge that she'd seen. How stupid.

'Oh well, please yourself, Isabel Williams.' I stalked off in a huff. I couldn't believe how ungrateful she was. And I thought she was a friend.

I was feeling so cross as I crossed the playground that I had to stop for a second and take a deep breath to calm down. I looked over my shoulder and saw Is was still standing exactly where I had left her, still kicking at bits of gravel. 'I don't know why I bother,' I muttered to myself as I started off again. Unfortunately, I was still looking at Is as I set off so

I didn't see Kevin Ryder coming in the opposite direction as he sauntered into the playground.

'Hey, watch where you're going!' he yelled as I careered into him.

'Sorry Kev, didn't see you there.'

'Want to watch where you're going mate,' he repeated. 'Anyway, it's lucky I bumped into you.'

'I think I bumped into you actually.'

'Don't matter. Lucky for you either way. I'm gonna make you an offer you can't refuse.'

'Sorry? I think you're wrong there, Kevin, whatever it is.'

'You seen The Godfather?'

'Whose godfather?'

'Not anybody's godfather. The Godfather. It's a film, just come out. It's about the Mafia, you know, organised crime and all that? You must've heard of it.'

'Oh yes, I think I have. But what about it?'

'That's where it comes from, see? The film: Marlon Brando in the film he's the Godfather and he says "I'm gonna make you an offer you can't refuse".' Kevin repeated it with an American accent so awful it made him sound ridiculous, not menacing as he intended.

Trying to keep a straight face, I answered. 'No, sorry Kevin, I haven't seen the film. In fact I don't think I can. I'm under age. How come you've seen it?'

'Well I haven't actually seen it, not properly,' he admitted. 'But my brother has.'

Kevin had an older brother who was in his final year at school, and was even bigger and uglier than Kevin, if that were possible. It was also why Kevin used to hang around with some so-called 'mates' who were a lot older than he was. I could see why The Godfather would appeal to him.

'You still haven't told me what you want, Kevin. What "offer" are you making exactly?' I asked.

'How would it be...?' he started, as he slid his hands into his pockets and leaned back in what he assumed was a nonchalant way. 'How would it be, if you didn't 'ave to do no more maths homework?'

'Great. That'd be really good. And you're going to do it for me I suppose are you?' I laughed.

'Yeah. You got the picture.'

I stared at him for a minute, wondering if my hearing was going.

'I think you'll have to say that again, Kevin. I thought for a minute you were saying that you'd do my maths homework for me.'

'Zactly,' he replied and a broad grin crossed his face, making him look like one of those pumpkins you get at Halloween.

'Well, it's a very nice idea, Kevin. Thank you. But isn't there something just a teeny-weeny bit wrong with your very generous offer?'

'What?'

'You're no good at maths.'

'Don't matter.'

'It does if I want my homework to be right.'

'That is the beauty of my little proposition.' He smiled again in a horrible, smarmy sort of way. 'What I'm offering you…'

'…this offer I can't refuse, you mean?' I added.

'Correct. What I'm offering you is the chance to have your maths and other homework done for you by the best brains in the school.'

'Not by you then?' I couldn't resist saying.

'No,' Kevin missed my sarcasm, 'course not, it'll be done by a team of experts carefully chosen from the top form in the school.'

'And who has chosen this team of experts? You?'

'Don't be daft,' Kevin laughed. 'Course not. They've been chosen by my brother. We call it Brains United!'

'Brains United? It's like Manchester United is it?'

'No, don't be stupid, that's a football team. No, Brains United is like bringing together all the best brains to work on your homework.'

'Really?'

'Yeah. My brother's mates do it for you, you see? I mean the maths we have to do is easy-peasy for them. They could do it standing on their heads.'

'Is that wise?'

He ignored this and carried on.

'So what do you think then? Worth every penny I'd say.'

'I wondered when you would get round to the cost, Kevin.'

'Well, you can't expect me to provide a service like that for nothing, can you?'

'Of course not. And so how much will it cost to have Brains United do my homework for me?'

'10p a week.'

'10p a week. You have got to be joking.'

'No. Why would I? I told you it was an offer you couldn't refuse. And if you want more subjects I can do you a deal.'

'I thought you said it was 10p a week to have my homework done?'

'No, 10p for maths. You'll have to pay extra for other subjects, course you will. I mean you could have Brains United Science...'

'Brains United Science – B.U.S. – that spells "bus" doesn't it?'

'Does it?' Kevin's brain cells worked overtime

and eventually he agreed with me. 'Oh yeah, so it does. Yeah, well, as I say there's that one... or you could choose Brains United Geography...'

'B.U.G. Bug.'

'Oh yeah! That's funny isn't it?'

'Hilarious Kevin. But I'm sorry, I really don't want to waste my money, thank you.'

'You don't know what you're missing.'

'Oh believe me I do. I think having your brother's mates doing my homework spells nothing but trouble. Talking of which, do you realise what Brains United Maths spells?'

'What d'you mean?'

'Just work it out. It sort of sums up what I think of your idea.' I smiled and walked off, leaving Kevin frowning as his brain cells started grinding into action. And at that moment, thankfully, the bell went for the start of school.

4
Under the River

I hardly spoke with Is for the rest of the day – I was still feeling annoyed with her – and it wasn't until we were getting our coats off the pegs that she came up to me with a sly sort of grin on her face.

'Rob,' she said. I should have known something was up; she hardly ever called me Rob even though pretty well everyone else in my class did. She seemed to prefer 'Robert', which I thought sounded terribly old fashioned.

'Yes,' I answered as petulantly as I could.

'Oh, don't be like that,' she said. 'I've got an idea.'

'Well?' I tried to sound totally uninterested.

'You know that bridge...'

'Yes.'

Then her face became wreathed in smiles.

'Oh, Rob, you are funny! I'm sorry, okay? I'm sorry I was so ungrateful this morning – really!'

'It's just that...' I began, 'well I couldn't understand your attitude, that's all. I mean there's this bridge, large as life, just like you drew. And you don't seem interested. If that had been me, I'd have taken it and rammed it right down old Phillips' throat, the way he went on at you.'

'You'd have a job!'

'You know what I mean.'

'Yes, but it doesn't matter. Really it doesn't. I don't have to prove anything to Mr Phillips. What's he know about bridges anyway?'

'Not as much as you, obviously.'

'Precisely.' The way she said the word sounded so smug that if it had come from anyone else I'd have thought they were being really big headed. But somehow, with Is, I didn't think that of her. Coming from her it was, well, very natural. She wasn't boasting, simply stating a fact.

'Like I said,' she continued, 'when that bridge was built, there were loads of people as stupid as Mr Phillips. They said the whole thing would collapse of its own accord, before a train even went over it.'

'But it didn't.'

'No, course not. It has the widest and flattest brick arches in the world. But it's been standing for more than 130 years, no problem. And it has to contend with much heavier trains too, far heavier than the ones it was originally designed for.'

I looked at her with a mixture of admiration and astonishment that she should know so much about something which seemed to me so unimportant.

'It's funny, you being interested in things like that, bridges and trains and all,' I said.

The minute the words passed my lips I regretted them.

She bristled. Her eyes darkened and her mouth set in a hard line.

'Why? Because I'm a girl? You don't think girls should be interested in "boys' things", is that it?'

'I didn't say that.'

'No, but it's what you meant.'

'That's not fair!' I exploded. How strange that I could lose my temper so easily with her. I never did with anyone else.

It was my turn to apologise.

'What's this idea you've got then?' I asked, remembering what it was she came over to say in the first place.

Her face brightened immediately. 'Come outside, I'll tell you there.'

'Why the mystery?'

'I don't want anyone to hear.'

So I followed Is out into the playground and we pulled on our coats. By then most of the class had disappeared off home. All except Clever Trev who was being a right toady and sucking up to Mr Bartholomew about something.

'Do you fancy bunking off tomorrow?'

'What?'

'Do you fancy…'

'Yes, I heard you. I mean, what are you talking about? Why? I mean where?'

'It's an idea.'

'Pretty stupid idea if you ask me. What's the point?'

'I want to show you something,' said Is. 'It's to do with the bridge. Except it's under the Thames, not over it.'

'What do you mean?'

'You'll see! Come on, say you will! It'll be exciting! It'll be much more fun than going to boring old school!'

'All right.'

What made me agree, I'll never know. Just the thrill of it, I expect. It was like a game, a dare. Isabel could be like that. Making me do things for the sheer hell of it. I would never have dreamed of bunking off school before I met her.

'Where are we going then?' I said, as we

walked across the playground towards the gates.

'Surprise.'

'Where will we meet?'

'Corner of Willis Road and Lavender Hill at eight-thirty. Oh, and you'll need some money, the place we're going to is in London.'

'London! Oh, no I don't think we should Is...'

'Eight-thirty, all right?'

The next morning I turned up as she asked. I didn't give a moment's thought to what excuse I was going to give Mr Gregory the next day. I was going on a mystery tour.

I'd had to borrow £1.50 from Mum, saying I needed it for a school trip we were going on. I'm not that good at lying, so when she started asking me about it I got flustered and said London, since at least that was the truth.

'But I've already paid for that,' she protested. 'I'm not made of money you know. Anyway, you're going to London next month aren't you – to the Science Museum?'

'This is for History,' I lied. 'It's another trip, I forgot about it until just now.'

'You seem to have an awful lot of school trips suddenly,' said Mum with a puzzled look on her face. 'And I suppose you'll want a packed lunch, won't you?'

'No, it's all right, they're providing it.'

'Providing it? They never usually do. Where exactly are you off to then?'

'Oh, some boring old museum, more than likely.' I tried to sound nonchalant.

That didn't convince Mum in the slightest.

'I hope you're telling me the truth, Robert.'

I think I must have blushed at that point, but she gave me the money anyway and I ran out the house shouting 'Thanks Mum'.

'You're late. I've been waiting for ages.' That was the greeting I got from Is.

'What?' Is was in one of those moods, I could tell.

'You said 8.30. It's nearly quarter to nine.'

'I had to borrow money from Mum, okay? It took time. Look, I can always just carry on to school you know.'

'No, it's... I thought you weren't coming that's all.'

Then she brightened up instantly as if she were suddenly a different person. 'Come on, race you to the station!'

The railway station was quite a long way by road, but there was a short cut along a path that ran through some allotments and over a footbridge leading straight to the station.

We got our tickets and amazingly a train turned up in about five minutes. But that was the only thing quick about it. It seemed to stop at every station all the way to London.

All the time I kept my head down in case I was seen by someone I knew. I found myself staring at the huge platform shoes (they must have been three or four inches high at least) of the girl sitting opposite me. In the 1970s shoes like that were the in thing; girls wore them with skimpy hot pants or mega-wide bell-bottomed trousers.

Another thing that was in fashion was smoking. Everyone seemed to do it and it was perfectly legal to smoke on trains and buses and anywhere. I really couldn't stand it or understand how anybody else did. Everyone apart from Is and me seemed to be smoking and it was really foul. I couldn't wait to get off the train before I suffocated. Eventually, however, it pulled into Waterloo where I found myself being dragged straight down the steps into the Underground. Is seemed to know exactly where she was going but to me it was a maze of tunnels. Talk about a rabbit warren, I would have been lost in two minutes had I been on my own.

We hopped on one train, only to get off at the next stop and rush along tunnels to get on another train. As each station name passed by I followed our progress on the map above the windows in the train.

Temple. Blackfriars. Mansion House. Cannon Street. Monument (for Bank). Tower Hill. Aldgate East. Whitechapel.

'We get out here,' announced Isabel. The doors slid open.

'Whitechapel, that's where Jack the Ripper lived in Victorian times, wasn't it Is?'

'Know him, did you?'

'Not personally, he was a bit before my time!'

'You're lucky,' she said.

'Yeah, must have been terrible around here then.'

'It wasn't all bad.'

'No, I suppose not,' I said as we got on yet another train, a really filthy old underground train going I didn't know where. I was beginning to regret coming with Is at all. I thought it'd be fun. But by now it struck me as totally pointless.

At that moment the train rattled to a halt and the doors opened with the 'psst' noise of air.

'This is it! Wapping!' Isabel sprang from her seat and headed for the door.

'This is what?' I answered, following her blindly.

'You'll see.'

We both jumped out on to the platform of Wapping station. It was unlike any underground station platform I'd been on before (not that I'd been on that many, I admit). But it was incredibly narrow, I know that. Probably no more than a metre and a half across – half the width of normal platforms.

'See?' persisted Is.

There was nothing to see. It was a filthy old underground station, that was all. Everywhere it was old bare brick, really ancient looking. And there seemed to be cables trailing in great loops along the walls, dozens of them.

Overhead the brick roof of the tunnel we were in was grimy black. It looked like it was covered with soot, which I suppose it could have been because they used to have steam trains on some of these underground railways. It must have been awfully old soot though because the trains have been electric for ages and ages.

The other funny thing about the station was this enormous tunnel we were in (a Wapping great tunnel you could say!), not like modern tube lines, which are in much smaller tunnels. And here we were facing the other platform, instead of staring at posters on the tunnel wall opposite like you usually do.

Right at the end of the platforms the tunnel divided into two and, as we were watching, a train came roaring out of the one heading back towards Whitechapel.

'What are we doing here, Is?' I shouted above the sound of the train braking.

'Come up here,' she replied and disappeared up some steps behind us. It turned out this was the Way Out – though you'd never have guessed. Like the platform the steps were narrow and, instead of going straight up, they snaked out of sight around the corner.

When we got to the top of the steps we emerged into a vast vertical shaft. It was like being inside a castle turret. In the middle were the lifts and I went over to them.

'Are we going up then?' I asked.

'If you like,' Is answered and I pushed the button to call the lift.

'No, not that way!' she laughed. 'Up the stairs!'

'Stairs?' I looked up dismayed. There were the stairs all right and Is was running up them like a rabbit.

I've seen stairs in tube stations before. They call them the 'Emergency stairs' because no one in their right mind would bother climbing them unless it was an emergency. They spiral up like a never-ending helter skelter.

The stairs at Wapping weren't like that. They went up one way, then the other, then like a spiral staircase for a bit; then a straight bit, and so on. Is clattered up them ahead of me and I realised she was far fitter than I was. Every now and then she would turn and laugh as I panted after her.

'Wait for me...' I gasped after a couple of flights.

'Come on slowcoach!'

'Oh, wait Is, please...'

'All right.'

When I got to her she was actually sitting down! They'd put a bench for you to rest on one of the landings and Is was stretched out on it with a broad grin across her face.

As I got to her she jumped up.

'Right! Ready for the rest are you?'

'Oh, do we have to, Is?' I groaned.

'No, not if you don't want to.'

'I'd rather not.'

'We'll go back down then,' she said.

'We should have got the lift in the first place, instead of climbing all these stairs.'

She looked at me amazed.

'What for? I don't want to go up the top. There's nothing up there. I just thought you'd like to see this shaft, that's all.'

What was she talking about? She thought I'd like to see a hole in the ground somewhere in east London? She must be mad.

'What do you mean? You brought me all this way to show me the bottom of a filthy old underground station? What's so great about that?' The whole day was a waste and I was starting to feel annoyed.

'It's not just a filthy old underground station. It happens to be very important.'

'What's so important about it that you drag me halfway across London, Is? Eh?'

'It's important to me.'

And then, before I could answer, tears began running down her nose and she tried wiping them away with her hand. But her hands were so dirty from the station that she left smears down each cheek.

I felt an absolute git.

'Come on, Is. Don't cry. Please.' I tried my best to console her. 'Come on, I'm sorry. If it's that important to you, tell me about it. Please.'

'All right,' she sniffed.

A minute later we stood right at the end of the platforms peering into the gloom where the horseshoe-shaped tunnel snaked away from us.

'You're looking at the first tunnel ever built under a river in the world,' announced Is proudly.

'Really?' I answered, not knowing whether to look impressed or not.

'It was a tunnel for foot passengers originally.

Then they used it for the trains.'

'Well, it's all very nice, Is, but I don't see why you needed to show it to me.'

'I told you, it's very important to me,' said Is, her forehead creased as she concentrated. 'My father built it, you see.'

'Your father built it?' I repeated. 'Don't be daft. He can't have. This tunnel must have been built years and years ago. You said that yourself.'

Is cut across me, repeating firmly: 'My father built it.'

'Your father? What do you mean, your father?'

'Marc Brunel.'

'Your father's not Marc Brunel. What are you talking about? Your father is Mr Williams.'

'Only in this life.'

By now I was beginning to get more than a little nervous at the way she was talking, I can tell you.

'You're not making sense. Really you're not. And, in any case, we ought to be getting back now. We never should have come here anyway. It wasn't a good idea.'

'But don't you see,' she said quietly, 'I'm Isambard.'

'What are you talking about?'

'Do you believe in reincarnation, Robert?' she asked in a very serious way.

'Reincarnation? What do you mean? Like being reborn as somebody else, you mean? I've heard about it I think. When someone dies, some people say their spirit or whatever carries on and is reborn in another body. Is that what you're talking about?'

'Sort of. Do you believe it can happen?'

'Well, no, not really. I don't think I believe it anyway.'

'You should.'

'Why?'

'Because I've been reincarnated.'

My jaw dropped open in total disbelief. I'd never heard anything so absolutely ridiculous before. But she said it so seriously, I didn't know what to do.

'What?' was all I could muster.

When she answered, she spoke very slowly and deliberately.

'I wasn't always Isabel Williams. I have simply been reincarnated in this form. I was born on the 15th of September 1959, that's exactly 100 years to the day that Isambard died. That's who I was in a previous life. And that, in truth, is who I still am.'

Then her voice took on a strange shrillness that I found very disconcerting.

'Don't you see, Robert, I am Isambard Kingdom Brunel.'

5
Father Figure

That night, when I got to bed, I lay awake a lot of the time thinking about Is. What was it with her? All this talk about Isambard Brunel was ridiculous. I really didn't think I could handle it.

My reaction to what she had said had been to burst out laughing.

Her dark eyes had narrowed and her lips become tight at that. Then she threw her head back and hurled angry words at me.

'That's it. Go on, laugh! Laugh your silly head off!'

In that confined space her voice had echoed up and down the tunnel. There had been a dozen or so people waiting for trains and they all turned and stared at us.

'Ssh!' I said. 'People are looking.'

I thought that would quieten her. But no, she turned round and faced the passengers down the platform.

'And what are you lot staring at?' she said in a forceful but controlled voice that made them all turn away instantly.

Luckily, just at that moment a train came in with a whoosh and we got on. We travelled back home from Wapping in silence.

Incredibly, the next day it was as if nothing had happened. I saw Is just as we were due to go into school.

'Hello,' she said cheerfully, 'got your story all sorted out have you?'

'Oh, yes, I think so. I was just going to say I was sick when I woke up, food poisoning or something.'

'Where's your note then?'

'I haven't got one. Have you?'

'Course.' And she pulled an envelope out of her blazer pocket. On it, in really posh handwriting, was written: 'Mr Gregory, St Leonards School'.

I was impressed. 'You never got your mother to write you a sick note, did you?'

'Don't be daft.'

'Well who did then?'

'I did, stupid.'

'You did?' I didn't believe her. I'd seen Isabel's writing many times by now and it was rather spidery and small. The writing here on this envelope was altogether grander with lots of swirls and flourishes: very adult I thought.

'You can't have.'

'Suit yourself,' she answered and carried on into registration. It was only then that it struck me that I was going to be asked for my sick note. I should have thought of that.

We got into our classroom about a minute before the black bat shape of Mr Gregory swept in.

'Ah!' he said, as he spotted Is and me. 'The wanderers have returned! And what excuses do you both have for not being here yesterday? Eh? Morgan! I'm talking to you!'

'Sorry, Sir,' I stammered. 'I was sick.'

'Sick! I bet you were. Sick of what? Sick of having to go to school, I suppose, eh?'

At that I went bright red. As I said, I'm really not very good at lying.

'No, Sir, I had food poisoning.'

'Food poisoning? A likely story! Where's your note?'

'I – er – forgot it, Sir.'

At this Mr Gregory swept up the aisle and pushed his fat face right up close to mine. Judging by the smell of his breath, he would never suffer from food poisoning: the germs wouldn't survive.

'Just make sure you bring it in tomorrow then, boy!' he hissed at me.

As his breath engulfed me, it was like I imagine drowning. I was fighting for air.

But then he turned to Is.

'And what about you, Isabel Williams? Did you go down with sudden food poisoning too?'

'No, Sir.' Unlike mine, her voice didn't quaver. It was clear and precise. She had changed so much from the tiny, shy girl who first came into the class only a few weeks back.

'Then why weren't we all blessed with your presence yesterday?' continued Mr Gregory.

'I had an epileptic fit.'

I looked over to Isabel in astonishment.

'You had what?' said Mr Gregory with obvious disbelief. 'And how long have you suffered from epilepsy?'

'For a year or two now,' replied Is calmly.

'I see. Your mother never mentioned it.'

'My stepmother,' Isabel corrected. 'And it's not a problem usually. I take these anti-convulsive tablets, you see. Only – I forgot to yesterday. And that's what happens.'

'Oh, really?' said Mr Gregory. 'And I suppose

you have forgotten your note too?'

'No, Sir.' She pulled the envelope from her blazer and handed it to him.

Mr Gregory wheezed slightly as he read the note then put it down on his desk.

'I see,' he said, clearly convinced. 'That seems to be in order. But your mother – er stepmother – should have let us know. We need to know these things. Just in case, you understand. Well I hope you're feeling better today, Isabel.'

'Yes, thank you, Sir,' she replied and I couldn't help shooting a grin at her.

'Right, the register and then to work!' said Mr Gregory.

Unfortunately our first lesson that day was English, which meant that we had Mr Gregory to start with. It seemed that every awkward question he could throw at me he did.

'What's the main difference between an adjective and an adverb?' he demanded.

'I – er – I don't know, Sir,' I stammered in reply.

And so it went on.

'I didn't know you were epileptic,' I said to Is as we stepped out into the corridor.

'I'm not.'

'But you told Mr Gregory...'

'What's it matter what I told him?'

'Oh I don't know what to believe with you,' I said, exasperated.

'And what's that supposed to mean?' She stopped suddenly, facing me.

'You know.'

'No I don't.'

'All that stuff yesterday about Isambard Brunel.'

'It's true.'

'You're this famous Victorian engineer reborn as Isabel Williams?'

'Yes.'

'His reincarnation?'

'Yes.'

'Well, I'm sorry but...' my words were cut short by the leering face of Kevin Ryder, who had come up behind us as we stopped.

'What you talking about flowers for?' he started.

'Flowers?' I asked, at a loss to know what he was talking about.

'Yeah, you were talking about carnations. I heard you. Gonna buy your girlfriend flowers, are you Rob?'

'She is not my...' I stopped myself from saying any more. 'And we weren't talking about carnations.'

'I heard you.'

'Actually we were discussing reincarnation,

Kevin,' chipped in Isabel. 'Do you know what that is?'

The blank look on Kevin's face clearly showed he didn't.

'No, I thought not,' Is continued. 'Well, Kevin, reincarnation is nothing to do with flowers. It is to do with the belief that when someone dies, their spirit lives on and can be reborn in another body. Do you understand?'

'Not really,' Kevin admitted, trying to grapple with the concept.

'No, I thought not,' said Is again. 'If you were reborn, Kevin, what do you think you would come back as?'

'I dunno,' he said frowning. 'Someone really famous I expect.'

'I think you're more likely to come back as an earthworm,' said Is triumphantly.

'Or a slug,' I added, laughing. But, seeing the look on Kevin's face, I stepped back quickly. I'd obviously gone too far.

'What you say?' he thundered, his hands folding up automatically into a tight fist.

'Nothing. Nothing at all, Kev.'

'Yeah, well you better not. You know what,' he added, 'I think you two are really weird.' And with that he sloped off down the corridor to our next lesson.

When Mr Cummings, the maths teacher, handed out last week's homework books, I discovered that Kevin had already put his homework scheme into action. Amazingly he must have managed to sign up about five people from the class to Brains United. But the scheme failed for one very simple reason: all the answers were exactly the same. Now that shouldn't have been a problem in a subject like maths where there is only one answer. Except that unfortunately all the answers Kevin's brother's mates supplied were wrong. Identically wrong. And Mr Cummings smelt a rat.

'It is quite apparent to me that five of you have colluded to do your homework, or have had someone do your homework for you,' he said as he threw the homework books back to the offenders, who struggled to catch them as they flew through the air. 'For your trouble,' he continued, 'you will each spend an hour each evening this week in a special homework class, where you will be supervised. And don't ever dare try this one again!'

He scowled at everyone in the class just to make sure that we all got the message and wouldn't even think about trying such a thing in future. I was astonished to see that Kevin himself wasn't among those who were caught. It was only later that I found out he had got away with it through his own stupidity: he'd copied down most of the wrong 'answers' wrongly.

Lunchtime couldn't come soon enough as far as I was concerned. I wandered out into the sunlight with three or four others, including Is. I was just about to set off home for a quick lunch when I spotted a woman walking up and down outside the playground looking very agitated.

'Oh, God, what's she doing here?' said Is. She instantly lost all the cool she had had when facing Mr Gregory. Now she was no longer calm and collected. Her face had gone really white, which made her dark brown eyes look almost black.

'Who is it?' I whispered.

'My stepmum, of course,' Is answered.

'Well, aren't you going to go over? She's looking for you I expect. Otherwise what else would she be doing here?'

'I don't know. And I don't want to know.'

'Oh don't be silly. She's probably got something to tell you. Go on, it might be important.'

'Let's go back inside,' was all she said, and she started grabbing my jacket. But too late: Is and I had been spotted.

'Isabel! Isabel! Over here!'

'You'll have to go now,' I whispered.

'Come with me.'

'All right,' I agreed.

With obvious reluctance, Isabel dragged herself over to her waiting stepmum, while I tagged behind.

She doesn't look so bad, I said to myself when we got closer. She seemed very out of place though, standing there outside the wire fence.

Whenever I had seen anyone's parents turn up at school before, they came in whatever clothes they happened to be wearing. My mother used to have an old pair of jeans and a sweater on most of the time.

Is's stepmum looked like she had gone to quite a lot of trouble. She had on a very smart blue dress with a fashionable grey raincoat and dark blue high heel shoes. Her face was all made up too and her hair fell in soft brown waves around it.

She had a naturally happy face, though. And as Is and I got to the fence, I could see she was smiling with relief.

'Isabel... Isabel, I came to see you. Are you all right, love?'

'Course I am.'

'Well, I didn't know, love. Running off like that this morning, you seemed so upset.'

Isabel said nothing in reply.

'And after what happened the other morning... I didn't know what to think.'

'I'm all right, okay?' said Is flatly.

'As long as you are. I do worry about you Isabel, you know that.'

'I know.'

'Good,' Isabel's stepmum smiled briefly. Then she looked at me.

'You must be Robert.'

I was amazed she knew my name.

'Er, yes,' I replied.

'Isabel has told me lots about you.'

'Oh,' I said.

She laughed. 'Don't worry. All of it complimentary I can assure you! Isabel was a little worried about coming to St Leonards originally, weren't you Isabel?'

'No,' she replied with a scowl.

'Of course you were, dear. You told me so.'

I saw Is squirm at this, not surprisingly, but Mrs Williams didn't seem to notice and carried on.

'So it's nice that she's got you for a friend, Robert. Very nice indeed. She doesn't make friends easily as a rule, do you Isabel?'

Mothers can be pretty insensitive I know, but talk about showing someone up. I really felt for Is.

'You must come over one day and have tea, Robert.'

'Pardon?' I looked at Mrs Williams dumbly.

'Yes, come over today if you like. After school.

Yes, that will be nice. You'd like that, wouldn't you Isabel?'

Is didn't reply so I had to.

'Well, thank you, Mrs Williams, that'll be nice,' I managed to say.

'Good, that's settled. I'll see you both later. I'm so glad you're feeling better, Isabel, you know that.'

Still Is said not a word in reply. Her face was set hard and her eyes went black as she stared after the disappearing form of her stepmother teetering off on her high heels.

'What's up with you?' I asked once her stepmother was out of sight.

'You know exactly what.'

'I wouldn't have asked if I did.'

'What did you have to go and say you'll come for?'

'To tea? Your stepmother asked me.' I couldn't understand why she was getting so worked up. But I felt myself getting angry.

'Look, just say if you don't want me to come! I don't particularly want to anyway. But I've said I would now!'

'Do what you like,' Is muttered under her breath.

After school I collected my stuff and went off to find Is. She was standing outside the double glass doors that led to the assembly hall.

'Ready then?' I asked as cheerfully as I could.

'Suppose so.' She was still in the same mood as she had been that morning.

We set off together towards Isabel's house in Walton Road without saying another word. Just past the pub there was a phone box so I went in and rang my mum to say I wouldn't be back for tea.

When I came out she was halfway down the road. I ran after her and caught up.

'You could have waited; I was only ringing my mum.'

She didn't reply. It was only when we turned into Walton Road itself that she spoke.

'That's our house there with the laburnum tree.'

Since I didn't know what a laburnum tree was and the road was full of trees anyway, this wasn't much help. But a minute later we were standing outside a typical 1930s semi-detached.

It was a bigger house than the one I lived in, with large bay windows and quite a good size front garden; unlike ours where you only had to take a couple of steps and you were on the pavement. There were daffodils poking up through the lawn and right in the middle there was a tree, which I took to be the laburnum.

Isabel gave me a quick backward glance and then walked up to the bright-red front door. As she approached it, it swung open and Is's stepmother stood there with a broad smile on her face.

'Hello, you're back earlier than I thought! Come on in, Robert, and make yourself at home!'

She went inside and down to a door at the end of the hall, while I followed Is into the front room.

'What do you want to do then?' she asked.

'I don't know.'

'I've got this new puzzle game that's really good. You could see if you could do it.'

'What do you do?'

'I'll show you.'

Is went out of the room and up the stairs to fetch it. A second later her stepmum came in.

'Tea won't be long, you two.' Then, seeing that I was on my own, she added, 'Oh, has Isabel deserted you already?'

'No, she's just gone upstairs to fetch a puzzle,' I replied with a smile.

'That's all right then.'

Mrs Williams sat down in one of the armchairs facing the fireplace. She smiled at me in a slightly nervous sort of way as if she didn't know what to say next.

I looked around the room, desperately searching for something to talk about. And then, on the mantelpiece, I saw a little porcelain ballerina. It had

obviously been broken and stuck together again –
not too well by the looks of it.

'Oh, you've managed to repair it then,' I
chirped, before realising what I was saying.

'Pardon Robert? Repair what? The ballerina,
you mean?'

'Er, yes,' I said, looking intently at my hands.
'Is must have mentioned it – er – got dropped.'

'In a manner of speaking.'

'It's nice,' I said, wanting something to say.

Mrs Williams' voice became very quiet as she
answered. 'It's – it was – quite beautiful.'

Her eyes became very soft. Then they hardened
and fixed on me. 'Did Isabel tell you it was broken?'

'Must have.'

'I see.'

I was so anxious not to say anything wrong that
I did exactly that.

'She said it was an accident,' I rushed on.

'Oh, did she?' replied Mrs Williams.

'She said he just kind of knocked it as he went
out that's all,' I lied.

A frown crossed Mrs Williams' face. 'He? Who
do you mean, Robert? Who did Isabel say knocked
over the ballerina?'

I'd obviously put my foot in it, but at this stage
I had no idea how.

'Mr – er – Williams of course.'

My reply evoked the kind of silence that is so acute, you can almost hear it. Then Isabel's stepmother spoke crisply and without emotion.

'There is no Mr Williams, Robert. Isabel's father died three years ago.'

The shock was like someone slamming a door in my face. It couldn't be true. What on earth was she talking about? Of course Isabel had a father. It was her mother who had died. This Mrs Williams was her stepmother. Her father had married again. That's what Isabel had told me. Why would she lie about something like that? But then why would Mrs Williams lie either? I was starting to feel really confused.

I remembered the first time Isabel had talked about her stepmother. 'She's a cow.' That's how Is had described her. But here she was: seeming perfectly reasonable. I stared at her in disbelief, searching her face, questioning.

'Are you sure that's what Isabel told you, Robert?'

I didn't know what to say. The last thing I wanted to do was drop Is in it.

'He died three years ago, Robert,' Mrs Williams repeated. 'Isabel was heartbroken. I don't think she's quite got over it even now.'

'I see,' I said glumly. I was just about to say

something else when, over Mrs Williams' shoulder, I caught sight of Is's face peering round the door. It was ashen.

She must have heard everything we had said. Her head darted back quickly and she ran back up the stairs.

The sound made Mrs Williams turn round.

'Isabel. Isabel, is that you?' There was no reply. Mrs Williams stood up and went to the foot of the stairs. I did the same, not knowing what to do.

Then, from one of the rooms upstairs, came an unexpectedly loud scream which soon subsided into sobbing, a terrible unrestrained sobbing.

'Wait here, will you Robert?' asked Mrs Williams and, without waiting for an answer, she ran swiftly up the stairs. She stood outside what was evidently Isabel's room and called out in a soft reassuring voice, 'Isabel, it's all right, love. No one's cross with you. Come back down and we'll forget all about it, okay?'

But there was no reply, except the sound of Is gulping for air between sobs.

'I'm sorry, Robert,' Mrs Williams called down to me. 'Another time, perhaps. Soon. There's nothing I can do at the moment. You understand?'

I nodded sadly and let myself out of the front door.

6
A Cause for Concern

'I thought you were having tea round at Isabel's,' said my mum when I got home.

'I was.'

'You must have gulped it down then.'

'I didn't have any. Isabel wasn't feeling well.'

'Oh, I'm sorry to hear that.'

She picked up the magazine lying open on her lap and started flicking through it again. I sat down in a chair opposite her and looked vacantly out of the window. It was still nice outside. The late afternoon sun was making the bricks glow on the houses over the road.

Maybe I should go down the road and see Brian, I thought. But I didn't move. I was thinking about Is. Why had she told me all those things?

She said her mother had died and her father

had remarried when she was four. But it was her father that had died. So Mrs Williams was her real mother, not her stepmother at all.

'Penny for them.'

'What?'

'Penny for your thoughts,' said mum. 'You looked miles away.'

'Oh, did I? I suppose I was.'

'Shall I get you some tea then?' she said, as she put her magazine down and got up. 'Or what about a drink and we'll both eat with Dad when he gets home?'

'Okay, yes.' I looked back out of the window, lost in thought again for a second. 'At least I've got a dad though. Isabel hasn't.'

A horrified look crossed my mum's face. 'What do you mean Rob? You mean he's died! But when? Oh, poor Isabel!'

'Years ago.'

'But...? What are you talking about, Rob? I don't understand.'

'Neither do I. I've only just found out myself. Isabel's father actually died three years ago and she lives with her mother on her own.'

'I thought she lived with her stepmother. I thought her mother died and her father remarried...'

'That's what I thought too. It's what she told me.'

'Why on earth would she say such a thing?' Mum shook her head in disbelief and disapproval. Then she sighed, 'Ah well, I'll make some drinks shall I?'

'If you ask me,' she continued from the kitchen, 'that Isabel lives in a fantasy world.'

That certainly seemed true enough. After all, if Isabel believing she was Isambard Brunel wasn't living in a fantasy world what was? Reincarnation indeed! Who did she think she was kidding?

Mind you, I had to admit she did seem to know an awful lot about Brunel. She must have seen a film or read a book or something – yes that was it. And all this about her father was just another fantasy.

It was then I realised another thing. It must have been Isabel who smashed that ballerina. Of course!

The blazing row had been between her and her mother, not between 'Dad and Penny', like Isabel had said. Next day when I got to school I was going to have a good talk with Isabel Williams.

As it happened, when I arrived at school the following morning, there was no sign of her.

'Isabel Williams,' called out Mr Gregory and, hearing no reply, he looked up.

'Isabel Williams,' he repeated, looking straight at her empty chair. He could see there was nobody there. Did he expect the chair to answer? How on earth he got to be a teacher I'll never know. He was like a dinosaur: an enormous lumbering body with a pea-sized brain. The thought of Brontosaurus Gregory made me giggle.

'Morgan!' The booming voice of Bronto stopped me mid giggle.

'Yes, Sir?'

'Something amusing you, Morgan?'

'No, Sir.'

'Then why are you giggling, may I ask?'

'I don't know, Sir.'

'"I don't know, Sir,"' Mr Gregory imitated me in a particularly silly voice.

Then he reverted to his normal silly voice: 'And I don't suppose you know where young Williams is this fine day either do you?'

'No, Sir.'

'Is there anything you do know, Morgan?'

I resisted the temptation to say 'No, Sir' once again and instead tried to look contrite.

At that Mr Gregory ignored me, thank goodness. 'Wilson.' he continued.

'Here, Sir.'

And so another day at school began...

* * *

Finally it drew to a close and I decided to go round to Isabel's on the way home to see how she was.

I was right at the corner of Walton Road and about to turn into it when I stopped. What was I doing? Is wouldn't want to see me and to be honest I didn't think I much wanted to see her at the moment either. She had lied to me about her father. She was always going off in a huff or something. In fact she was acting pretty weird all round. And yet...

Talk about being indecisive. I started down Walton Road, then stopped, retraced my steps and stood again on the corner. I must have done that three or four times before eventually I found myself standing on the other side of the wall from the laburnum tree.

Well I was here now, I reasoned, and quickly walked up the path to the door before I had a chance to reconsider. I rang the bell and it opened almost straight away. Isabel's mother didn't look anything like she had two days ago. Her hair was tied back roughly with an elastic band and she had no make-up on. And it looked to me like she had been crying because her eyes were all puffy.

She wasn't wearing the smart clothes I'd seen her in before. Now she had on a pair of scruffy trousers miles too big for her and a t-shirt with paint on.

'Oh, hello, Robert,' she said as she recognised me. She didn't smile, but then she didn't seem particularly put out either, just sort of neutral.

'Hello, Mrs Williams,' I replied.

'Sorry you caught me doing the decorating,' she explained as if an explanation was called for. 'We're doing Isabel's room, you see.'

As she spoke she wiped both her cheeks with the back of her hand, not realising it had green paint on. The two streaks left by her hand made her look like a Red Indian.

'I'd invite you in, but we're right in the middle of things, you see,' she continued.

'That's all right,' I said, 'I was just wondering if Is – Isabel – was okay.'

'Yes, yes, she'll be fine. Bit of an upset that's all. She'll get over it, don't you worry. That's why we're doing her room. Take her mind off things. Doesn't do to brood on things, does it?'

'No,' I agreed. 'She's all right then? She'll be back at school tomorrow will she, only I feel sort of responsible, somehow, you know?'

At that Mrs Williams' face looked sad and happy at the same time. She sniffed as she smiled.

'Come on, there's no need for you to feel that, Robert. Don't be daft. It's something Isabel's got to come to terms with herself.'

'Maybe I could have a talk with her then? Is she here?'

'Not right now. We're in the middle of things anyway.' Mrs Williams turned on a pleasant but false-looking smile. 'You'll see her at school tomorrow; you can talk to her then. She'll be there, don't you worry.'

That part was certainly true. Is was at school when I got there. She was in the corner by the school tennis courts talking to Veronica Biggleswade. But the minute she saw me crossing the playground towards her she turned her back on me.

'Please yourself,' I muttered under my breath and changed direction to go towards the main entrance. I had my hand out to push the door open when my name was called out.

'Rob! Oi! Over here!'

I looked round to find Kevin Ryder smiling at me from a crowd of older boys, most of whom I only knew by sight.

I walked over, uncertain as to what Kevin Ryder could possibly want with me. I thought I had made my feelings towards him as plain as I could but then, as I've said before, he does have particularly thick skin. In fact he's pretty thick all over.

'Yes?' I asked with as much annoyance in my voice as I could manage.

'We've got a little proposition for you, Rob,' said Kevin gleefully.

'Proposition?'

'Me and the boys here are forming a group!' he announced.

'Group?'

'Yeah you know, like music.'

'Music?'

'Why do you have to keep repeating everything I say?' asked Kevin, beginning to become annoyed himself.

'Yeah, why do you have to keep repeating everything Kev says?' repeated one of Kevin's extra thick mates. Two Short Planks I called him.

'I'm sorry, I don't know what you're going on about,' I replied truthfully.

'Me and the boys here are forming a group.' Kevin said once more. 'We're going to make records and things, you know.'

'But you can't play an instrument, Kevin,' I said with great difficulty – trying not to laugh in his face.

'Don't matter.'

I knew I'd regret asking, but I did anyway. 'Why doesn't it matter?'

'I'm the lead singer!'

That did it. I nearly doubled up. I could feel my

face twitching and I began making strange guttural noises as I fought to hold back the roar of laughter ready to burst from inside me.

Kevin looked confused.

'What's so funny?'

I looked at Kevin and then at his large mates from the upper forms.

'Nothing,' I said with a reasonably straight face. 'Just a joke I remembered.'

Luckily Kevin didn't pursue it; he was much keener on getting to the point of his little chat.

'Thing is, all we need is a few more quid and we'll be able to get all the gear we need. That's why we thought of you. It's like an investment, you know. You put your money down and then when we make a fortune you get a share.'

'No thanks,' I said as politely and firmly as I could.

'Kev's offering you a share in our group,' said Two Short Planks.

'Well,' I smiled, 'thanks for the invitation, but no thanks.'

'Kev wasn't asking you if you wanted in or not,' Two Short Planks persisted. 'He was telling you.'

'I see.' At last I began to understand. I looked from one member of Kevin's 'group' to the next.

And the next. They were all as ugly as each other and all were expecting an answer. The question was how much did I value my face? A few pence seemed a small price to pay to keep my nose intact.

'How much?' I asked.

'Two pounds,' answered Kevin with a smirk.

'How much?' I was aghast. Two pounds may not seem like much now, but back in the early seventies it was quite a lot of money and a lot, lot more than Kevin's last scheme – Brains United. You could buy an album for £2 – by someone decent. So paying two quid to have Kevin Ryder and his Morons inflicted on everyone hardly seemed like a bargain. Nevertheless I dug deep into my pockets, but only came up with 85 pence, some creased picture cards, some sticky sweet wrappers, two sticks of Wrigleys, a button and lots of fluff.

'You'll have to do better than that,' said one of the other members of the group, pounding one fist rhythmically into the flat of his other hand. I figured he must be the drummer.

'It's all I've got,' I said in an alarmed voice. 'I can get the rest for tomorrow.'

'Make sure you do,' was the only answer I got. And then, relief of reliefs, the bell went to signal the start of school.

I rushed inside without another word. Isabel

must have slipped by me while I was having my little chat with Kevin and his mates. When I got into Mr Gregory's class she was already sitting, grim-faced, at her desk.

'Ah you're back with us today are you, Isabel? Good. Good,' remarked Mr Gregory when he looked up. 'Not another fit I hope.'

'No, Sir.' Without saying another word she got up and went over to his desk, nearly being knocked over in the process by Kevin as he tore into the room.

'Not so fast, Ryder!' yelled Mr Gregory, and amazingly he managed to catch Kevin by the back of his shirt as he tore past. For a glorious moment I thought Mr Gregory had choked him, but no such luck.

Kevin managed a squeaky 'No, Sir' and continued to his desk at a snail's pace. Then Mr Gregory turned his attention to Is.

'Right, have you brought a note?'

She pushed her hand into a blazer pocket and pulled out a crumpled envelope which she handed over. Mr Gregory ripped it open and looked at the letter with a frown on his face.

'This is from your mother, is it Isabel?'

'Yes, Sir. Of course it is – Sir,' replied Isabel. I was pleased to see that she was back to her old stroppy self.

'Then what has happened to her handwriting?' wheezed Mr Gregory. 'Why has it changed so dramatically from the last note you brought in, eh?'

'I don't know.'

'You don't know! YOU DON'T KNOW! You're as bad as Morgan. He doesn't seem to know anything either. But I'll tell you this my girl...' He tapped the letter angrily with his podgy fingers. 'This letter here is a forgery!'

He stood up, raising himself by his fists from the desk, and his face was bulging. Isabel looked really scared.

'No, Sir,' she said in a very quiet voice.

'Yes, Sir!' bellowed Mr Gregory. 'Yes, Sir indeed! I know a child's handwriting when I see it.'

'I didn't write it Sir.'

'No, one of your horrible little friends did, I've no doubt. You forget, Isabel Williams, I've seen your mother's handwriting. Proper handwriting it was, when you brought in her note last time. Why you can't even think of a decent excuse, can you? 'A little upset,' it says. 'Please excuse Isabel for not being at school yesterday, she was a little upset.' What rubbish! I'll give you upset, my girl.'

And with that he screwed the note up into a tight little ball and threw it into the big bin by his desk.

'Write out "I must never forge sick notes in future" two hundred times. Then we'll see what your handwriting is like won't we?'

Mr Gregory sat back on his seat with a smug smile of satisfaction on his face. I looked over at Isabel and gave her what I hoped was a reassuring look.

7
Another Piece of the Puzzle

For the rest of that week and virtually all the next I hardly saw anything of Is. She was there in the classroom for lessons but the minute we got outside she disappeared. It was obvious she was avoiding me. Couldn't bear the fact that she'd been found out lying I suppose. Though I couldn't blame her really. I'd have done the same in her position.

I may not have seen much of Is but I saw plenty of Kevin. After I managed to come up with two pounds, he started treating me like one of his mates, which was really horrible. As an investor he said he owed it to me to keep me informed as to his group's progress. It turned out that he had managed to get two pounds (and sometimes more) from half the class. I wouldn't have been at all surprised if he hadn't managed to get 'investments' from half the school. He certainly raised a lot of money, because within a couple of days he proudly announced he'd bought a new guitar.

'So your little investment's starting to work, isn't that good?' he said smugly.

I couldn't see what was so good about having helped buy him a guitar.

'Yes, terrific, Kevin,' I replied in a bored voice. 'In any case, I thought you were the lead singer of this group. What do you want a guitar for?'

'Adds to the effect doesn't it?' he said as if I knew nothing. 'Don't you know nothing?' he added.

I resisted the temptation to say that I knew what he could do with his new guitar and there would be no shortage of people willing to help him shove it there. Instead I said I'd have to come and see him play some time, to see how my 'investment' was coming along.

'Good idea! Why not?' He leapt at this, which made me think how stupid I was for suggesting it. 'We're having a rehearsal on Friday night in the old scout hall, you can come then!'

'Oh, great, thanks.' I accepted the invitation without enthusiasm, not intending to go.

But Kevin invited everyone else who had been coerced into putting money into his group. By Friday everyone I talked to seemed to be going to the rehearsal. So what else could I do but join them? At least we'd all have a laugh at Kevin's expense.

As it happened, we didn't even get that. Against all expectations, The Strangers, as they were called (not Kevin and the Morons, after all), turned out to be pretty good. I even had to admit that Kevin could sing. Although he did look pretty ridiculous with a guitar round his neck that he never once attempted to play...

The other major surprise of the evening was that Isabel was there. How Kevin managed to persuade her to part with two quid as an investment I'll never know.

She was leaning against a pillar in the corner of the hall when I went over to her.

'Didn't think you liked this sort of music.'

'I don't.'

'Kevin get you to invest too then did he?'

'Yes.'

'Looks like he got most of the school.'

'Mmm.'

'Still, it's not as bad as I thought it would be.'

'No, surprising isn't it?' She smiled and looked away.

When she turned back her face was serious.

'Sorry.'

'Sorry for what?'

'You know, telling you all those things. I can't help myself.'

'Forget it.'

'No, it's just that...' At that point whatever she said was drowned out by Kevin screaming 'Come on baby I want you so bad' into a microphone, followed by an horrendous squeal of feedback.

'Come outside!' I yelled above the cacophony. 'We can talk outside.' Silently Is followed me into the car park.

'It's just that...' she began.

'Yes?' I prompted.

'I've never spoken about my dad before, not really.'

'You miss him a lot, don't you?' I asked gently.

'Yes. I think that's what turned me against Mum.'

'How?'

'Oh, Mum's not so bad, but she does fuss. All the time. Like an old hen. It gets up my nose. And when – when Dad died she became totally overbearing. I couldn't stand it. She was trying to step into his shoes as well. And she couldn't. That's when I started thinking of her more like a stepmother than my real mum.'

'But why did you tell me your father was still alive?'

'He is still alive – to me anyway.' Her mouth sank into a sulk and she turned away to face the wall outside the hall. Behind her head someone had scrawled on the brick: Help preserve wildlife – pickle a squirrel, which made me smile.

'It's not funny,' Is countered, seeing my grin.

'It wasn't what you said,' I mumbled, feeling foolish.

Is peered at me then, unblinking. Her dark brown eyes searched my face as if she didn't know whether she could trust me or not. I got the impression she was turning things over in her mind, wanting to say something but not knowing whether she dare.

'What is it?'

'Nothing.'

'Come on, try me.'

'Dad was an engineer too you know. Sort of runs in the family, you see.' She permitted herself a slight smile at this remark.

'What did he do?'

'Nothing very grand. He worked for a small tractor company. He didn't design anything. Nothing like that. All he did really was put other people's ideas into practice.'

'Still, it takes skill to do that.'

'Oh, yes, he had a certain skill all right. He didn't

have an actual talent for engineering, that's all.'

'Like Isambard you mean.'

'Isambard had genius.'

'Well, yes of course,' I agreed.

And inwardly I felt enormously relieved. At last she seemed to be talking about Brunel in much the same way I would – in the same way anyone would.

Finally I thought I'd got to the bottom of it. All her talk about being Brunel was tied up with her father's death. The profound effect it had had on her was probably what started her off.

She obviously wanted her father to be something more than he was. 'Nothing very grand' was how she had described him. So more than likely this stuff about Brunel being reborn as Isabel Williams was a way of compensating for what her own father hadn't achieved.

'That's the reason then, isn't it?' I said, before I could stop myself.

'What's the reason?'

'You know: your obsession with Brunel. It's because of your dad.'

Is looked at me with a mixture of horror and hate on her face.

'It's okay,' I said quickly. 'Don't worry, I understand.'

'No you don't. No you don't. Nobody does.'

She turned and walked away. I watched her disappear down the street, thinking how totally, absolutely stupid I was. One day I'd learn to keep my mouth shut.

Then someone opened the door of the hall to leave the rehearsal, and the strains of Kevin and the Morons (sorry, the Strangers) burst on to the pavement like a drunk being thrown out of a pub.

* * *

There was the school trip coming up in the next few days – to the Science Museum in London. I wanted to go to the Natural History Museum where they have the dinosaurs. There I could see one of Mr Gregory's ancestors I thought – Brontosaurus Gregorius himself.

But the Science Museum it was.

My mum was very sceptical about it. 'You won't be having a school trip to London every week will you Rob? You're more out of the classroom than in lately.'

'I know,' I admitted.

'Well I don't mind,' she continued, digging in her handbag for some money, 'but it gets a bit expensive you know.'

'I doubt there will be any more trips this term,

Mum,' I reassured her. 'It's just that there's something special on at the Science Museum this week.' I'm glad she didn't ask me what, because I didn't have the faintest idea.

'Everybody's going,' I added cheerfully as she dropped some coins into my hand.

As it was, not everyone in the class did go. At the last minute, John Carter managed to get a severe nose bleed. Nobody found out how. All he would say was he had walked into a door post. I took him down to the Deputy Head's room to see Mrs Pearson, the nurse.

'Come on,' I said as we walked down the green-and-cream-painted corridor, 'you can tell me, it wasn't a door post was it?'

'I can't stand that sort of music, you know I can't,' was all he could splutter through the red-stained handkerchief. 'Give me Mozart any day.' Ah, well I thought, but look where it got you – preferring Mozart to the Strangers...

I hurried back to find everyone in the classroom waiting for me. Mr Phillips was drumming his fingers on the desk and weaselly Mr Bartholomew, the history teacher, was standing nervously next to him.

'Come on, Morgan, I don't know why it takes you so long to do things. You're too slow to catch a cold you are,' said Mr Phillips in his usual grumpy way.

'I came as quickly as I could,' I protested. 'We had to wait for Mrs Pearson.'

'Yes, yes. Well, you're here now, so let's all get going, shall we, or we'll miss the train.'

The train was pretty well empty. There were a couple of women chatting at one end of the carriage and two or three businessmen quietly reading their newspapers. Not for long.

A group of us piled in and all round one unfortunate businessman, our parkas flapping round us, taking up the whole carriage. He was reading the Financial Times, which looked really dull. We started talking about interesting things like music and football in our normal loud manner, which annoyed him no end. I bet he was reading the same paragraph over and over again with us talking across him – especially as we kept having to lean out to look round his paper to see each other.

He started making grunting huffy noises and then, in an exaggerated way, he started opening his newspaper right up each time he wanted to turn a page, which with a paper the size of the Financial Times meant he needed half the carriage.

Even that didn't have any effect on us. After a while, he let out this enormous grumpy sigh, screwed his paper into an untidy ball, stood up and got his briefcase from the luggage rack. He went down the other end of the train where Veronica Biggleswade, Isabel and the other girls were. Not that they were behaving any better.

He finally got off; slamming the door shut in fury, while we carried on to London and caught the tube. It was packed so most of us had to stand. We had a great laugh trying to stay upright without holding on and then being thrown from one side of the carriage to the other as the train rattled along. At one point I was thrown backwards and about eight of us went over like dominoes. I went sprawling over the dirty wooden floor.

'For goodness sake,' yelled Mr Phillips above the noise of the train, 'hold on would you!'

As I picked myself up I caught sight of Is.

'You okay?' she asked with a smile on her face.

'Oh, yes, course.' I replied, trying to brush off my blazer and grab hold of a handrail to haul myself up at the same time.

I made it back to my feet and stretched up to reach one of those hanging grips they have in tube trains. Isabel, I noticed, was only holding on to the handrail lightly with a thumb and finger.

'You must have good balance.'

'Oh, I've had plenty of practice,' she answered.

I knew then that what had been said the night of Kevin's rehearsal was now forgotten and we were friends again. But, more than that, she was acting as if nothing had happened at all – just like before. It was very weird the way she could just switch on and off like that.

Finally the train slowed down and clattered its way into the next station. As the signs saying South Kensington came into view, Mr Phillips leapt up. He had been first on the train and grabbed a seat before anyone else had had a chance.

'Right, this is it! Come on you lot, hurry!' he called. 'Or the doors will shut on you.'

'Yes, get a move on,' added Mr Bartholomew.

To get from South Kensington station to the Science Museum means walking down this ridiculously long tunnel. It starts from inside the station and then runs along under the street somewhere until you come up some steps right by the museum. At least you wouldn't get wet if it rained.

But it's really boring, there's nothing to see except endless tunnel, covered in brick-shaped cream tiles. It's only every now and then that you can catch glimpses of the outside world through sort of windows above your head.

But as soon as we set off along the tunnel we

discovered the one good thing about it was the echo it made. We clattered along the concrete floor making as much noise as we could with our shoes. Some of the boys had metal tips and they were really good, ringing and echoing the whole length of the passage.

'Can you all try to walk a little quieter?' yelled Mr Phillips above the clatter.

'Sorry, Sir, we'll try, Sir!' we yelled back in unison, making as much noise and additional echo as we could.

'Then please do,' said Mr Bartholomew, who was nothing if not polite. 'Or I shall have one of my headaches.'

'Poor old Digger. He has terrible trouble with his headaches,' I said to Is, who was clattering along beside me.

'Digger? Who's Digger?' she replied.

'Mr Bartholomew,' I explained.

'But why "Digger"?' she whispered.

'Because his name is James C. Bartholomew – JCB,' I answered with a grin.

She still didn't understand.

'His initials are JCB. Get it?'

She obviously didn't because she just shook her head in puzzlement and carried on walking. We passed signs saying to the Natural History Museum where I really wanted to go, and to some other museum, but on we trudged.

Up ahead there was a busker playing an acoustic guitar and singing this Bob Dylan song really badly. So badly it made Kevin sound absolutely amazing. Thankfully he stopped playing as we went past, which was a great relief. No doubt he figured it wasn't worth wearing his fingers to the bone for us. There was no way we were going have enough money to drop it in his guitar case.

A few minutes later we came to the end of the tunnel. Mr Phillips stopped by some steps and pointed up them.

'Okay, you lot, this is it, follow me!' And we all trooped up behind him, squinting into the bright sunlight.

We turned right at the top of the steps and there we were – at the entrance to the Science Museum.

8
Big is Beautiful

In we all went, through the large glass doors of the entrance hall. Mr Phillips went up to someone dressed in a uniform, who kept looking over at us while nodding at something Mr Phillips was saying to him.

We just hung around taking it all in. I'd never been to the Science Museum before so I didn't know what to expect. Clever Trev, needless to say, reckoned he'd been loads of times. He was probably born there.

'Right, we'll go through here first,' announced Mr Phillips. 'Follow me.'

So, with Mr Phillips at the front and JCB at the rear we marched through the Science Museum. Whenever we got to a particularly uninteresting pile of junk, Mr Phillips would stop and point enthusiastically at it.

'Ah, this is a particularly interesting exhibit, isn't it Mr Bartholomew?'

'Mm yes,' JCB peered at it inquisitively.

'It's a pump, probably for pumping out the water from mines. Driven by steam as you can see.'

'A Watt is it?' asked Trevor Smart, smugly.

'A steam pump, Smart. I just told you. You should wash your ears out.'

'No, I mean is it a Watt steam pump? Ah, it is, there's the label: "Boulton and Watt". See?'

'Oh, right. Yes, quite correct Smart.' Mr Phillips sounded pretty narked at Trevor outsmarting him. 'Yes, this was made by James Watt, inventor of the steam engine. Has anyone heard of James Watt before?'

'I have, Sir,' yelled out Clever Trev, his glasses steaming over with excitement.

'I know you have, Smart. Anyone else?'

If anyone had they weren't letting on. Nobody bothered raising their hands at any rate. But that didn't stop Mr Phillips going on and on. Listening to him was really mindnumbing. He could probably patent himself as a cure for insomnia.

'Here, you see, as that piston is forced in and out by the pressure of steam it pushes that arm there, which causes that huge wheel to rotate. What do you think of that? Morgan?'

Personally I thought it would be a good idea if Mr Phillips was under the huge wheel as it rotated, but I guessed that wasn't the answer he was expecting.

'Wow,' I said.

'There's no need to be cheeky, Morgan,' said Mr Phillips curtly. 'Right, well, let's get on. There's much more to see.'

A chorus of groans met that remark, but on we went. The next room had loads of old trains in it. There was one called the Rocket which JCB nearly wet himself over, he was so excited. I couldn't see why. Rockets were things that a few years before had landed on the moon. This rocket looked like it would have difficulty making a landing on a scrap heap.

Opposite it was a really enormous green steam engine. It was pretty impressive, I'll give it that. The wheels alone were much taller than me.

'Caerphilly Castle,' said Isabel as she came and stood beside me.

'Yes, I know,' I replied. 'It's got the name there, over the wheel.'

'Beautiful isn't it?' continued Is, and she seemed quite lost for a second.

'Well, I wouldn't go that far,' I laughed. 'It's only a steam engine.'

'No, you're wrong there, Robert,' was all she replied.

It was a funny thing with Isabel. If it had been Mr Phillips or JCB waxing lyrical over a large lump of metal I'd probably have nodded off. But with Is, I found myself drawn in. Somehow she made me see things differently. Perhaps it was because she had such a direct way of speaking it made what she said seem so much more important.

I noticed she almost always looked straight at you when she was speaking too. Most people look away every now and then. Is didn't. She watched your face intently with her dark brown eyes. It could be very disconcerting.

'It's from the Great Western Railway.'

'I know that too,' I replied, trying hard not to sound as smug as Clever Trev. 'It says it there on that truck.'

'Tender,' she corrected me. 'It's called a tender.'

'Tender, then.'

I ran my hand along one of the solid steel bars (connecting rods, so Is informed me) that joined together the enormous wheels we were standing next to.

'Anyway,' I conceded, 'I suppose it's more interesting looking than the average InterCity train. Seems a lot bigger than a modern train too.'

'No, it's not. It's just that you don't usually see trains from this angle. You're normally on the platform.'

'I suppose you're right. I never thought of that,' I said, continuing to run my hand over the metal.

Suddenly I realised that the whole surface had been covered with grease. My hand was disgusting. 'Oh, yuk, it's all greasy!' I moaned, turning round as I spoke. 'Just look at my hand.'

But Is wasn't behind me as I thought. Instead I found myself staring into the beaming face of Kevin Ryder.

'Your hand's all dirty,' he said, stating the obvious.

'I know.'

'That's a steam engine, that is,' he continued.

'No? Really?' I answered as if surprised. 'Is that what it is? I thought it was a fire engine.'

This remark took a while to permeate the deep recesses of his skull. But finally he managed to set his razor-sharp brain to work.

'No, don't be daft! Can't be. Fire engines are red! Don't you know nothing Morgan?'

''Spose not,' I answered and walked straight past him towards where the rest of the class were. As I went by the front of the engine, I saw Isabel. She was standing in the tracks right in front of the

Caerphilly Castle.

'See this...' she said.

'What?'

'You were saying how much bigger this looked than a modern train.'

'Yes?' I replied, wondering where this would lead us.

'It could have been much, much bigger, you know.'

'It could?'

'Mmm, this track here is what they call standard gauge.'

'So?'

'Well this is the track width that most railways have now. But imagine how much bigger trains could be if the rails were wider apart. They wouldn't only be bigger; they'd be a lot faster, smoother and loads more comfortable.'

'Why aren't they then?'

'Because the people who built most of the railways last century couldn't see beyond the end of their noses, that's why. They really thought that laying tracks this wide was good enough. What idiots!'

The way she spat out the word 'idiots' quite alarmed me. I could see that she was starting to get carried away again but I made no attempt to rejoin the rest of the class. Instead I found myself watching her mouth intently as she spoke.

'Only one railway company realised how much better it would be to have a wider gauge. And that was the Great Western. It was originally built with tracks seven feet wide. Can you imagine that? But because all the other railways were like this, the government passed a law that made the Great Western reduce the width of its tracks.'

'That's stupid.'

'You're telling me. That was one battle I lost.'

'What do you mean "one battle you..."' I started saying and then realised what she meant: it was one battle Brunel had lost. That again! The thing with me finding out about her father hadn't changed anything after all. I watched her eyes carefully, looking for clues as to what she was really thinking.

Just then, Kevin went past again and caught sight of us both there between the tracks. A horrible, slimy grin slid over his face.

'Hello, what're you two up to then? Having a little cuddle by the choo-choos are you?'

I went bright red. Even though I saw a lot of Is, I'd never thought of her as a girlfriend. She was just another mate really.

'Quiet snog is it?' Kevin persisted.

Is's face hardened and she gave Kevin a look

that would terrify the toughest of criminals. Then her face softened and she smiled sweetly.

'I'm sorry I told you you'd probably come back as an earthworm if you were reborn, Kevin.'

'That's all right,' Kevin said, scratching his head. He obviously didn't have a clue what she was on about.

'No it's not,' she replied. 'It's totally unfair to earthworms. After all, the common earthworm certainly has a lot more virtue than you.' Kevin stared at her, his eyes blinking, not really understanding what she was saying, as she carried on, 'I should go away, before I crush you under my heel, you disgusting, ridiculous little boy with your filthy little thoughts. You are quite beneath contempt.'

I gaped at her, and then Kevin.

Kevin looked totally shocked. He stood there, his mouth flapping, with no words coming out. He almost looked like an earthworm. He gave Is and me one last startled look then squirmed and slithered off towards the rest of the group. I burst out laughing.

'Well that'll teach him!'

'He's a total waste of oxygen.'

Then she caught hold of my hand. She had never done that before. I just hoped Kevin didn't see us.

'Come this way,' she said and pulled me through the gap between the Caerphilly Castle and a bright blue diesel engine next to it.

'But we ought to get back to Mr Phillips,' I protested.

'Not for a minute. He can wait,' was all she said.

She let go of my hand then and I followed her round the back of the engines. I could hear Mr Phillips chuntering on, somewhere on the other side. We came to some stairs, at the top of which was a sort of balcony which overlooked the rest of the hall. From up there I could see Mr Phillips pointing madly at some old car with most of the class gathered around.

A few others were with Mr Bartholomew looking at an old bicycle, which struck me as a really ridiculous thing to do, but that was old JCB all over. And Clever Trev was completely on his own talking to one of the Science Museum attendants, boring him rigid no doubt.

It was then I recalled something my father had said, that day we went out for a walk: 'That bridge at Maidenhead I saw. That was on the Great Western Railway too, wasn't it? My dad said so.'

'That's right.'

'So was it built for those wider tracks you were

talking about then?'

'Of course. The whole route was laid out for broad gauge. It was the straightest, flattest, fastest, most perfect railway ever built.'

'Oh, only that good,' I laughed.

She ignored me and carried on. 'Most of the route from Paddington to Bristol was completely level, or as good as. It was only when we got close to Bristol that there were any hills at all, like at Box.

'Box? What Box?' Cardboard box, wooden box, I wondered.

'The great tunnel at Box. It's on a 1 in 100 incline. Box,' she added, seeing I was still confused, 'is a place.'

'Of course it is,' I said, trying to make out I knew all the time.

'It's near Bath.'

'Oh, right.'

'It's nearly two miles long, eight times the length of the Thames tunnel. And, when it was finished, Box tunnel was the longest tunnel ever built. It took more than two and a half years to build.'

'Slow workers were they?'

'I'm being serious, Robert.' And she was. When Is was like this, she was in no mood for jokes or sarcasm.

'The men had to dig it with picks and shovels

and blast through the rock with gunpowder. They got through a ton of gunpowder and a ton of candles every week.'

'What did they need candles for?'

'To see by, of course. The whole tunnel was built by candlelight – that's all they had. At one point towards the end there were 4000 men and 300 horses labouring night and day on it to complete it on time.'

'And was it?' I asked.

'What?'

'Completed on time?'

'Oh, yes,' she said with what seemed like real pride in her voice, 'in June 1841. But the most amazing thing of all is that, on the 9th of April – if you look from the west end at dawn – you can actually see the sun rising through the tunnel.'

'Really? How?'

'The tunnel is aligned exactly with the position the sun will rise that day. It's the only day of the year that it does that. Isn't that amazing?'

'Well, yes, but I don't understand; what's so special about April the 9th?'

'It's my birthday.'

'No, it's not. You told me your birthday is September 15th.'

'Isambard's birthday. You know what I mean.'

'Then why did you say it was your birthday?'

'It is – in a way.'

'Look, Is – Isabel – you can't go on like this. You've got to get out of this believing you were someone else. Really you have.'

'I can't "get out of it", as you say.'

'Why ever not?'

'Because it's true!'

I sighed heavily. This was ridiculous. What was happening to her? She just seemed to be getting more and more obsessed with this Brunel thing.

'Come on upstairs then. There are some other things you must see.'

But I decided enough was enough. 'I think we should stay with Mr Phillips,' I said firmly. And only then did I realise that Mr Phillips, JCB and everyone else had gone.

'Come on Is, we'd better catch them up,' I said, in a panic.

'Why?' she answered, 'it doesn't matter. We can catch up with them later. They won't miss us.'

'Of course they will, don't be daft.'

'Oh, come on, Rob, this won't take two minutes.'

And once again, against my better judgement I allowed myself to be taken in by Is and led up two sets of escalators to the second floor.

There was absolutely nobody else up there

when we got there. And not surprising. Here there were more models in glass cases. But boats this time. Just boring old boats. Did they have something to do with Brunel too, I wondered. More than you could ever imagine, of course.

Is led me straight over to a model of this old-fashioned-looking boat with a funnel as well as masts for sails. It was called the *SS* Great Britain. The plaque above it told me what I'd already guessed.

'So Brunel built boats as well, did he?'

'Designed them, Robert. I didn't build them. The men did that. And it's a ship, not a boat.'

'Designed ships, then.'

'Yes.'

'And I suppose they were bigger and better than anything else around at the time too?' I asked, with more sarcasm in my voice than I really intended.

'Of course...' She walked over to another model. 'But this... this was to be my greatest triumph...'

I went over and looked through the glass at a strange-looking ship which had masts for sails, large paddle wheels on the side, plus a propeller and five funnels. It was a monster, no doubt about it.

Above the model there was a plaque, which I read out aloud: 'The Great Eastern, 1858. The largest vessel afloat from 1858 to 1899. A ship some forty years in advance of her time in size and design.'

'That's what finally killed me.'

I looked at Is in astonishment. Her face was reflected in the glass and those penetrating eyes of hers still seemed to be looking at me through the reflection.

'What finally... killed you, Is?' I asked nervously.

'The strain of it all, of course. The Great Eastern was just too big a project, even for me. I was never that strong you know... I used to be terribly ill as a child.'

'Oh, come on Is, what are...' but, before I could say another word, a woman's voice on the PA system interrupted me.

'Will Isabel Williams and Robert Morgan please make their way to the entrance hall where their teacher is waiting for them. I repeat, will...'

'I told you we shouldn't have come up here, didn't I?' I yelled, making for the stairs. 'Come on, get a move on; Phillips will be in a right state.'

9
Sink or Swim

It was about a month before the name Brunel cropped up again. Things had been going okay. I had been spending more time with Brian down the road but I had been round Is's a good few times too, and things seemed a lot better there.

Her mother was more relaxed and I didn't sense that funny atmosphere you sometimes get in places where everyone's on edge. It seemed really fine. My mother got to know Is's mother too and they started seeing each other quite often and going out shopping together.

One night, Isabel and I went along with a whole crowd to see Kevin and the – sorry, the Strangers – do their first real gig; it was at a local youth club, but I suppose everybody's got to start somewhere.

When we went in there was only a record player going. It hardly made enough sound for anyone to hear, even though it was on full volume.

By the door there was a hatch where they were selling Coke, coffee and packets of soggy crisps and where everyone was hanging around.

At the other end of the hall was the stage. It was really tiny and had tatty crimson-colour curtains hanging down either side. It was difficult to imagine how Kevin and his mates would all get on stage together; especially as what little space there was had been filled with these enormous black speaker boxes.

The Strangers also had these lights which flashed in time with the music; at least that was the theory. They seemed to have a mind of their own and flickered on and off wildly whenever there was a lull in the music. I found out later that Kevin had roped in Clever Trev to do the lights, so I can't say I'm surprised at how useless they were.

Still, there were loads of people there and at the end they even got some applause. Personally I think it was just that everyone like me had been conned out of money by Kevin and his band of upper-sixth thugs. And we were hoping if the Strangers did well we might see our 'investment' back some time. Fat chance.

Kevin even had this idea of performing in a concert the school was talking of putting on at Easter. The fact that the musical *Jesus Christ Superstar* was on in London at the time may have had something to do with it.

I think Kevin probably saw himself as some sort of Andrew Lloyd Webber figure. The mind boggles. But luckily the idea didn't get off the ground, so we were spared that spectacle.

So, as I say, all in all things weren't too bad. But then, just as we were going along nicely, what happens but another science lesson with Mr Phillips...

'Today we're going to learn a bit about how water behaves,' started Mr Phillips as he walked up and down the aisle. He was behind Jamie Johnson, one of Kevin's mates, at the time.

'Johnson, perhaps you'd like to tell the class what you know about water?'

Jamie had to twist his head round to look at Mr Phillips, who was now hovering ominously above him. 'It's wet, Sir?'

We all giggled at that. All except Mr Phillips, of course.

'Very good, Johnson. And what do you use it for?'

'Washing? Sir?' I sensed Jamie was cowering

slightly as he gave his answer, not quite sure if it was the right one.

'Washing? Yes, very good Johnson! But tell me...'

'Yes, Sir?' Jamie was relaxed now that he thought he'd got it right; not a good idea when Phillips is around. He had no sooner got the words out than he found himself pinned to the desk with the full weight of Mr Phillips on his shoulders and the obnoxious breath of Mr Phillips hot in his ears.

'If you know about washing, Johnson, tell me, why is your neck so disgustingly filthy!'

Mr Phillips strode back to his desk amid howls of laughter at Jamie's expense.

'But we are not here to discuss the sad state of young Johnson's neck,' he continued. 'I have something else here which might amuse you.'

With that he reached under his desk and brought out a brick, an ordinary brick. Well, half of one. He put it on the desk with a dramatic thump. For a minute I thought he might pick it up and aim it at one of us. But no, he opened a drawer and took out a reel of cotton which he proceeded to tie round the brick. Then he held the cotton up so it was taut, and looked round the class.

'Okay, who would like to try and lift the brick with this piece of cotton.'

No prizes for guessing whose hand shot up first. Well actually, his was the only hand that was raised.

Mr Phillips beamed. 'Ah, Smart! You fancy a go, do you?'

'Yes, Sir,' replied Clever Trev as he got up from his desk.

Despite valiant efforts by me and a couple of others, nobody managed to trip Trev up on his journey to Mr Phillips' desk.

'So you think it's possible to lift this brick without breaking the cotton do you?'

'Yes, Sir.' Clever Trev naturally thought there was a trick and for some reason the brick would lift. He didn't realise he was being set up.

'Well let's see you do it then.'

Oh, how Trevor's face was contorted with concentration as he gradually increased the strain on that slender thread of cotton.

And how Trevor's face was a mixture of anger and disappointment as the cotton parted with a twanging noise!

Oh, how we all giggled! Even Mr Phillips had to suppress a smile.

'Right, now let's try it another way.'

He went over to the side bench where there was a fish tank full of water and brought it back to his desk. Then he tied a fresh piece of cotton to the brick and lifted it gently to the bottom of the fish tank. The end of cotton trailed up and over the side.

'Who would like to try to lift the brick now?'

Nobody, it seemed.

'Right, Ryder, up you come.'

'Oh, Sir...'

'Up you come.'

Kevin Ryder got heavily out of his seat and shuffled towards the front of the class.

Really, with the three of them all there together, Mr Phillips, Kevin Ryder and the brick, I found it difficult deciding which was the most intelligent. Eventually I came down on the side of the brick. It was definitely the one with most personality.

But, surprisingly, Kevin's demonstration was very convincing. He lifted the strand of cotton and gently pulled on it. To our amazement, the brick lifted up in the water.

Mr Phillips smiled again. 'Thank you, Kevin.'

Kevin Ryder swanked all the way back to his seat with a broad grin on his face. It must have been the first time that he had actually managed to do something right. Still, we didn't begrudge him his moment of glory. He'd made Trevor Smart look pretty silly after all. Although Mr Phillips obviously had a lot to do with that too.

'Now, who knows why that happened?' he asked. 'Have any of you any idea why Trevor was unable to lift the brick without the cotton breaking, yet Kevin managed to?'

'Sheer brilliance?' suggested Emily Ford, who had a bit of a crush on Kevin. She also needed glasses.

'Unlikely,' replied Mr Phillips, which was a rather kinder remark than usual for him. 'The reason why it was easier in the water is because the water was helping to lift it too.'

He demonstrated lifting the brick again as if waiting for a round of applause. We didn't oblige.

'You see? What's happening is that the water is exerting what we call an upward thrust on the brick, trying to lift it. And what's amazing...'

(...is that I'm still awake, I thought.)

'... is that the upward thrust is equal to the weight of the water that the brick has displaced. Isn't that incredible?'

'Incredible' certainly wasn't the word I'd have used.

But Mr Phillips was in his element. 'This principle was first discovered by a Greek mathematician called Archimedes who lived thousands of years ago. He discovered it while having a bath one day. He noticed the way that the water rose when he got in and then worked the rest out in his mind.'

None of us, it seemed, had the faintest idea what Mr Phillips was rabbiting on about.

'He was so excited he ran straight out of the house into the street, without any clothes on, yelling "Eureka!" "Eureka" means "I've found it!"'

We perked up a bit at that.

'I bet he had!' smirked Kevin and some of the girls started giggling.

'Thank you, Kevin,' Mr Phillips said as reproachfully as he could. 'The point is you can see now why you were able to lift the brick and Trevor wasn't, can't you?'

If Kevin could see, he wasn't letting on. So Mr Phillips turned his attention to Jamie.

'And you, Johnson, what do you make of it, eh?'

Jamie gave a blank look in response.

'Well,' Mr Phillips continued, with a big grin on his face, 'I should try it if I were you Jamie. You could make a major scientific discovery lying in your bath! Who knows, you might even discover soap!'

There was a sort of wheezy sound like an old donkey braying. It was Mr Phillips laughing at his own joke while his bald head bobbed about under the glare from the spotlight.

Still laughing he carried on. 'And this of course is the reason why boats float. After all, metal doesn't naturally float does it? I mean, if you put a bar of metal in a bowl of water it'll sink, won't it? But, make it into a boat shape, and it doesn't. That's because there's an upward thrust lifting it, equal to the weight of the water the boat has displaced.'

As you can imagine, most of us just let his words wash over us.

The exceptions were Clever Trevor, who tried sucking up to Mr Phillips by asking questions and appearing interested, and Is, who was sitting bolt upright and had an intent expression on her face.

'When we go on a ferry we all accept that it's made of metal, don't we?' Mr Phillips went on. 'We don't give it a second thought. But we should stop and ask ourselves why it floats, shouldn't we?'

'Because the ferry company'd be sunk if it didn't,' chortled Kevin, obviously still flush with the success of his brick levitation.

Personally I thought that was quite good for Kevin, but Mr Phillips was less than impressed.

'Yes, thank you, Ryder. You can keep your jokes to yourself in future.' After a pause while he wiped his shiny bald bit with a handkerchief, Mr Phillips carried on. 'Of course, when they made the first iron boats, back in Victorian times, people didn't believe they'd float either. In fact, some of you may remember a couple of years ago they brought back one of those early iron boats from the Falkland Islands, way down near the tip of South America.'

We all looked blank. I didn't remember anything about any iron ship. And at the time the Falkland Islands meant nothing to us either; after all, the Falklands war didn't happen for another ten years.

'The ship,' blabbered on Mr Phillips, 'was the SS Great Britain...'

My ears pricked up at that. The SS Great Britain was one of those boats Is had shown me in the museum. I looked across at her and grinned at the happy coincidence. But she didn't appear to notice me. She was staring straight ahead, in a way I knew spelt trouble.

'... at the time it was one of the largest iron ships ever built...'

'It wasn't one of the largest, Sir. It was the largest,' interrupted Isabel.

'All right Isabel, it was the largest. That's hardly important, is it? The fact that it was a bit bigger than other ships of the time is of no consequence.'

'It is of great consequence to me, Sir, it most certainly is,' replied Is firmly in a suddenly very adult and formal-sounding voice.

Mr Phillips looked taken aback by the way she had answered him, but before he managed to say anything, she continued in the same vein.

'And I will have you know that the Great Britain was not – to use your inadequate words – "a bit bigger than other ships". She was, Sir, at 3444 tons, twice the the size of her contemporaries.'

Mr Phillips recovered himself to say with a smirk: 'Yes, well thank you for the history lesson, Isabel. We'll let you know when we want to find out some more.'

Is continued as if she hadn't heard a word he said.

'People said that it would sink, of course. There are always sceptics in every society. Always there are those who cannot, who will not, believe. I had to suffer more than my fair share of such fools.'

'I hope I don't have to repeat myself, Isabel. I seem to remember you adopting this ridiculous tone once before in my class. Well I have to warn you, I will not have it.' Mr Phillips was quite clearly bristling by now. But Isabel took no notice. She carried on as if there was nobody else in the room.

'The SS Great Britain, of course, was nothing compared to my final triumph,' she said. 'I was determined to launch the greatest ship in the history of mankind. And I did!'

'Ssh,' I whispered at her and shook my hand from side to side to try to make her stop. But she wouldn't, she was completely oblivious of everything around her.

'The Great Eastern was to be that ship. And I, Isambard Kingdom Brunel, was the engineer to design it.'

'Shut up, Is!' I hissed. But it was too late; everyone started giggling. Mr Phillips tried to restore order.

'Okay, that's enough, Isabel.'

She obviously didn't hear him.

'The Great Eastern was not merely a very great ship. She was, Sir, at 692 feet long, twice the size of anything else afloat. Six times the size of my own Great Britain. That is why we had to launch her sideways. She was far too long to launch in the normal manner.'

'I said you can stop,' said Mr Phillips loudly.

'Why, the hull alone weighed more than 12,000 tons. She had room for 4000 passengers and 3000 tons of cargo. No other ship could compare with her. Nobody had ever attempted to move such a weight before.'

'Will you shut up!' Everyone went deadly quiet as we realised that Mr Phillips was about to blow up. Everyone, that is, except Isabel.

'It took months to launch the great ship. Months! I poured my soul into that ship, my life. I do believe that is what finally killed me. I was mentally and physically drained by the effort. The strain was too much for me. It was forty-nine years before there was a ship to compare to her. I think sometimes perhaps the Great Eastern was too big, too far ahead of her time.'

'Be quiet, Isabel!'

Then she slowly got up from her chair and stood very stiff and erect, gazing at Mr Phillips.

'I will not have the likes of you telling me to be quiet, Sir. No, Sir, I will not have it! I will have my say.'

'I've had it up to here with you, Isabel. I can hardly believe what I'm hearing!'

'Naturally you cannot, Sir. As I said before, there are always sceptics, those who refuse to believe. And you, Sir, can be numbered amongst them.'

I think the only reason that Mr Phillips didn't do anything for a second or two was that he was so flabbergasted at Isabel's cheek. Then his eyes starting bulging and his mouth began twitching madly, and he took in a huge breath while clenching and unclenching his hands.

Finally he raised himself from his desk and

screamed so loudly that Mrs Potter, who was teaching French in the next classroom, came rushing in to see what was the matter.

'GET OUT GETOUT GETOUTGETOUT GET OUT!!!'

I thought for a minute he would explode and there'd be bits of Mr Phillips dangling from the striplights. But no such luck. Mrs Potter stood there at the door, horrified, as Is scuttled through the gap, tears streaming down her face.

10
Is is Gone

And that was the last Mr Phillips or St Leonards ever saw of Isabel Williams. She ran straight down the corridor and out of the side door. Mr Bartholomew happened to be coming in as she was rushing out and the door slammed in his face.

'Ow! What the...' he yelled. 'Come back here, I say, come back here when you're told!'

But Isabel was already out of the school gates and halfway down the path. Within a few minutes, most of Class 2F was out by the door too, staring with a mixture of disbelief and admiration at the fast-disappearing speck that was Isabel as she ran off down the road.

Mr Phillips, needless to say, was absolutely fuming. In fact I don't think I'd ever seen him quite so mad as he was that day. He could hardly contain his anger. He stood there growling and sucking in air between his teeth with a horrible murderous look in his eyes. And whenever anyone said anything to him he practically bit their head off.

Finally, after a few minutes of watching nothing in particular, he told us all to get back to our classroom.

'Come on, the show's over,' he said, with a menacing tone in his voice. 'I'll deal with Miss know-it-all Williams later.'

Mr Bartholomew was still nursing a sore hand where the door had smashed into it. Mrs Potter hadn't the faintest idea what was happening.

'Will you please explain to me why Isabel ran out like that?' she asked Mr Phillips in her peculiarly high-pitched voice.

'None of your business,' he snapped and pushed past her.

'Oh!' she exclaimed, very put out indeed. 'How dare you speak to me like that, Mr Phillips? How dare you?'

'Don't you tell me what I dare, Mrs Potter. Don't you... dare.'

He stormed back to the classroom with all of us trailing behind, grinning all over our faces. What wonderful excitement! And, needless to say, it took Mr Phillips ages to calm down. I think there was still steam coming out of his ears at the end of the lesson, he was that mad.

He told us all to open our books and read about a rotten old experiment we were supposed to be doing. No one, but absolutely no one, was to talk. Not one word. Or their life wouldn't be worth living.

I don't think anyone could have learnt the slightest bit from the rest of that lesson, we were all wondering about Isabel. I couldn't concentrate on anything; that was for sure.

When the bell finally went to signal the end of the torture you couldn't see Class 2F for dust.

'Where'd she go? I hope she's all right,' said Veronica, voicing what we all felt. Well, what most of us felt anyway.

'You know I always thought she was a bit touched, that Isabel. Bit weird I reckon. Know what I mean?' said Kevin.

'Kevin,' I found myself saying, 'why don't you stuff a sock in your gob?'

Luckily for me Kevin realised he was in the minority and, since he didn't have Short Planks or any of his other ugly Neanderthal mates with him, he instantly shut up. I never knew I could have such an effect on people. Mind you, even if he had hit me I don't think I'd have cared just then. All I wanted to do was get round to Walton Road and check that Is was all right. The end of the day couldn't come quick enough.

But come it did and I dashed down the path and across the road, narrowly missing being knocked down by a car that I hadn't even noticed.

By the time I got to the laburnum tree, I could hardly speak, I was so out of breath. My heart was thumping and I had that pounding in the ears that you get when you've been running really too hard.

Everything looked completely calm and quiet. I had expected there to be some sort of commotion going on, but there was nothing.

I went up to the door and rang the bell. I waited, trying to get my breath back.

No reply.

I rang again, with desperation in the way I pushed the button.

Still no reply.

Then the neighbour's door opened and a woman (Mrs Higgins her name was) stuck her head out.

'She's gone out.'

'Where?' I gasped, still fighting for breath.

'Dunno. Like I say, she's gone out.'

Suddenly I resented this nosy woman with her ghastly nylon floral housecoat and her hair bound up under an equally horrendous bright headscarf.

She looked at me with little piggy eyes like Mr Phillips too.

'Well you're a fat lot of help, aren't you?' I shouted at her, and instantly I knew I shouldn't have. Mrs Higgins opened her mouth to say something then changed her mind, stared at me for a second, and disappeared back into her house, slamming her front door shut.

At that moment a ginger cat appeared and started rubbing itself around my legs. It never knew how close it came to being booted over the garden wall...

With no other ideas, I set off dejectedly for home. After running all the way to Isabel's I took my time walking back, partly to get my breath back and partly because I wanted time to think. When I came to a bus shelter I sat down on the seat, swinging my feet to and fro and looking at the cracks in the pavement. It just seemed to me that life was so horribly unfair. Why should Mr Phillips and people like him get away with being so foul? I couldn't understand it. And where on earth could Mrs Williams have gone with Is?

By the time I finally got home it was much later than usual. I shuffled up to the door, aimlessly.

'Where have you been?' said my mother, the minute I opened the door. 'We've been worrying you'd gone too.'

'Gone where?' I asked, perplexed.

'Why, with Isabel of course,' replied Mum, 'Mrs Williams is in the sitting room.'

She opened the door and there was Mrs Williams, sitting opposite the fireplace. I could see her eyes were all red as she looked up when we entered.

'Hello, Robert.' She tried to smile at me, but failed miserably.

'Hello Mrs Williams.'

'Have you any idea...?' she asked. 'We thought you might know where Isabel might have got to?'

'I didn't know Isabel had gone anywhere,' I answered truthfully. 'I've just come from your house. I went round to see if she was all right, after what happened.'

'What did happen, Rob?' asked my mother.

'Oh, she had this big bust-up with old Phillips, that's all,' I said. 'She ran out of the classroom. But we all thought she'd gone straight home.'

'When I got home, I found this,' said Mrs Williams. And she handed me a tatty piece of paper torn from a school exercise book.

On it, in Isabel's handwriting, was a short note: 'Mum, I'm going away and I won't be back. I can't stand things any longer. I've gone somewhere where I will be welcome, Isabel.'

There was no 'Dear Mum' or 'Love Isabel' or anything like that. The handwriting was strange too. It was definitely Isabel's but parts of it were like the handwriting she'd done when she wrote her sick note the time we bunked off school, all swirls and flourishes.

I handed the note back to Mrs Williams with a sick feeling in my stomach.

'I... I don't know where... where she could have gone, Mrs Williams. I'm sorry...'

'You're sure now?' asked my mother in a more aggressive tone than I could ever remember her using.

'Of course I'm sure,' I yelled angrily. 'Of course I am.'

'All right, all right, calm down,' said Mum. 'We're all worried, I know. But I'm sure she'll turn up soon. I expect she'll be back when she starts feeling hungry.'

'You don't know Isabel,' replied Mrs Williams.

How true, I thought.

'Well, she can't have got far. But we ought to let the police know, oughtn't we? Just to be sure, don't you think? Should have done that straight off really. Come on Penny, I'll come with you.'

'Are you sure?' asked Mrs Williams, wiping her cheek with the back of her hand as I had seen her doing once before.

'Of course.' Mum went out and got her coat. 'Robert,' she called from the hall, 'you'll be all right here for a bit won't you? If Isabel turns up, just make sure you keep her here, okay?'

'Of course I will.'

'Right, well you know where we are...' and with that, Mum ushered Mrs Williams out of the front door and into her Mini.

They drove off down the road with a great crashing of gears while I went up to my bedroom to reflect on these latest developments.

* * *

I think everyone really expected Is to reappear the next day, like my mother said she would. But when she didn't, we started getting more worried.

The police turned up at school without warning the day after that. Kevin went visibly pale when he saw the police car drawing up outside the school. I wondered what it was he had to hide exactly...

But they hadn't come for Kevin. They'd come for Mr Phillips, although not to arrest him, more's the pity. They just came to talk to him to see if he could shed any light on Is's disappearance.

Needless to say, he couldn't.

By the end of the week, Mrs Williams was at

her wits' end. And when I got home one night and picked up the local evening paper, it was full of Is's disappearance. There, right in the middle of the front page, was a picture of Is staring out at me. The way she looked it seemed as if she was pleading to be left alone. 'I don't want to be found,' she appeared to be saying.

There was a long interview with Mrs Williams. It wasn't the first time Isabel had run away, apparently. She'd done it twice before. But she had always come back within a day and usually she turned up at a friend's house, which was why Mrs Williams came straight round to us I suppose.

It seemed they had lived all over the place too. First they were somewhere near Manchester. That's where they were when Is's father died. Then in London for two years and for a while they lived down in the West Country with relations. But, according to Mrs Williams, she was hoping that this time they would stay put. She thought Is was much happier than she had been. And then this happened...

Dad said he didn't think the police were doing enough. Someone must have seen Is or given her a lift or something. But it was as if she had simply disappeared into thin air.

As you can imagine, life at school was even

worse than usual. Everyone went round with long faces. Well, that's a bit of an exaggeration, but you know what I mean. Even Mr Gregory and Mr Phillips turned almost human for a while. I expect they thought it was somehow their fault. I certainly hope so. With luck they had really rotten nightmares. That'd teach them. It was time they were taught something, instead of inflicting their stupid lessons on us all the while.

One evening I remember was particularly horrible. I had got home and had my tea early because I was planning to go round and see Brian a bit later on, after I'd finished a plastic ship model I was building.

I was in the sitting room, fiddling with part of one of the masts that wouldn't fit, when a voice from the corner brought me up sharp.

'Today the body of a young girl was discovered in woods near Basingstoke,' it said. 'The body, which has not so far been identified, was found by a walker who noticed a torn fragment of a red plastic mac caught on a nearby bush...'

Red plastic mac? Did Is have a bright red mac? I stared at the television set in horror.

'The girl, believed to be around twelve years old, had been brutally attacked and the body has several stab wounds...'

I felt sick. Surely it couldn't be? It mustn't.

'The police are appealing for information. Anyone who was in the vicinity in the last two days is asked to contact their local police station or the Basingstoke police on...'

I didn't know what to do. More in anger than anything else, I rushed over to the television and thumped the switch off. Then I tore upstairs to my bedroom and threw myself on the bed. I could feel that prickly sensation you get in your eyes just before you cry.

But I didn't cry. Instead I thumped the pillow with all my might, nearly splitting the material with my fist.

'Rob, whatever's the matter? What has got into you?'

I looked over my shoulder to see my mother framed in the doorway. Her face was pained and concerned.

'What is it?' she repeated.

'Nothing... oh, it was just something that was on television, that's all.'

'What? What was on television?'

'On the news. They say they've found this dead body – of a girl – she's Is's age.'

'It's not Isabel, is it?'

'I don't know: that's the point.' And with that

I couldn't hold the tears back any longer. I blubbed like a baby and Mum came over and put her arm around me, holding me tight.

'It's all right. It's all right. We'll find out. But I'm sure it's not Isabel, they'd have said. Come on, Love, there's nothing we can do about it at the moment, really there's not.'

Reluctantly I allowed myself to be led downstairs and sat in one of the armchairs. Mum went off to make some tea and came back a few minutes later with a steaming mug in her hands.

'Here, have this. And take these too.'

She held out two aspirins or paracetamols or something.

'I haven't got a headache.'

'They're for tension.'

I took them and swallowed both together with one gulp of the hot, sweet tea.

'Better?'

'Don't feel any different.'

'You will.'

And surprisingly I did. And later on I heard that it wasn't Is that they had found at all. It was some other poor girl. They had an interview with her parents too; the mother could hardly speak, she was so distressed. It was really painful to watch.

Yet at the same time I felt a huge wave of relief

that it wasn't Is – and then felt immediately guilty for being so callous.

It made me think, though. While I was safe and secure at home, Is could be anywhere. Anything could happen to her. She had to be found. Someone had to find her and I knew who that someone was. Me.

11
Thumbs Up

It was at the end of the second week after Is had
gone that it came to me. What had she said in her
note? 'I'm going somewhere where I will be
welcome.' That was it.

But where could she go at this time of year? It
wasn't exactly hot at the beginning of April, after all.

I was in the kitchen eating my cereal and while
I was thinking I was looking at a calendar my
mother had on the wall. On it was a picture of a
tiny cottage in the country, all wreathed in roses
and what they call picturesque. But I wasn't looking
at the cottage. I was looking at the date: Friday
April 7th.

And then something Is had said to me came
rushing back: '...it's the only day of the year that it
does that. Isn't that amazing...?'

Of course! Sunday was the 9th of April. Isambard Brunel's birthday. The day that the sun is supposed to rise through that tunnel at where was it? Box. At Box! That's where she'll be. The more I thought about it, the more convinced I was. I remembered the look on her face when she told me the story.

'Of course...' I said out loud, without meaning to.

'What, dear?' asked Mum as she reappeared with the morning's post.

'Oh, nothing... anything good in the post?' I asked, trying to change the subject.

'Bills by the look of it,' she replied going through them. 'And more bills,' she added disgustedly.

'Oh.'

'What's the time, anyway? Come on, Rob, you'd better eat that up and get going. You'll be late for school otherwise.'

'So?'

'Don't start that attitude, Rob. You've got to go to school, you know you have.'

'Isabel's not.'

'That's a different matter. Now come on, get a move on.'

So I shovelled the last of the Frosties into my mouth and grabbed my blazer and satchel.

On the way down the road to school I realised

I couldn't tell my parents what I suspected. It sounded too bizarre for words.

As I walked a plan began to form itself in my head. I would get down to Wiltshire somehow the next day. Then I would only have to find a place to stay for one night and I could turn up at the tunnel on Sunday morning...

At dawn...

I shuddered at the thought of having to be up so early. Still, it would be worth it. I knew it would.

I wondered what to say to Mum and Dad. What could I say I was doing? Perhaps I could say I was staying with a friend for the night, I thought. No, I didn't know anyone that lived more than a few roads away really.

I'd just have to leave a note and make my own way. At least it would say I was coming back, not like Is's note. Anyway, if I left late afternoon or early evening I could travel through the night. So I'd hardly be away for more than a few hours when you come to think of it...

As long as I went when Mum and Dad were out it'd be no problem. I knew that on Saturday afternoons Mum would be out shopping and Dad often popped round the corner to his friends in Warwick Street, but I'd still have to be quick.

So that Saturday I went off with some friends

to the recreation field for a game of football in the morning and then after lunch told Mum I was going to have tea with one of them.

Instead I came back around half past four. As I let myself in the front door, there was no sign of Mum. 'So far, so good,' I said to myself as I headed for the kitchen.

Opening a wall cupboard, I grabbed a couple of packets of biscuits, some crisps and a Mars Bar. I didn't know Mum even bought them. Then I saw a Swiss roll, so I swapped some biscuits for that. There were some apples and bananas in a fruit bowl on the windowsill, so I chucked them in too.

Then I thought about clothes. I went into my bedroom to get a jumper, which I threw into the duffle bag together with a pair of socks for good measure. Though what I thought I needed with a clean pair of socks I have no idea. I never normally bothered with such things.

I crept back down the stairs and was just about to let myself out of the door when I started having pangs of doubt.

Was this stupid or what? I mean, what was I doing rushing off like this, to somewhere I'd never been before, just on a hunch that Is would be there? What if something happened to me? I should tell them I was going, shouldn't I? But how could I?

The minute I said where it was, they'd be down there like a shot and we'd lose the chance of finding Is. In my muddled brain I reasoned that the only way was for me to go on my own.

I got out my dad's map of south-west England and pored over it, looking for this place called Box. I found Bristol easily and then Bath, but no Box. Finally, after staring at the map until my eyes started going funny, I methodically followed the railway line with my finger until I came to it. There it was!

I stuffed the map into my duffle bag and then grabbed an old coat. It was only at that point I realised I had nothing to sleep on. Upstairs I ran again and pulled open a big drawer under one of the wardrobes to get the sleeping bag I knew was there. But it wasn't.

I was starting to panic a bit now. I looked at my watch. Five o'clock. Mum would be back soon. I had to hurry. Looking at my watch reminded me I would need an alarm clock too.

No time. No time...

I tore into the spare bedroom. Maybe they'd put the sleeping bag in – yes, there it was, pushed on top of the wardrobe. I stood on the bed but couldn't reach it and, in desperation, started jumping up and down to try to grab it.

On the third attempt I caught a corner and dragged it with me to the floor.

Quickly I rolled it up and tied it with one of my belts. Then I remembered the alarm clock and grabbed the little black battery one by my bed.

Anything else? A note. I must leave a note...

I settled for just leaving a short message – just enough to put their minds at rest:

'Dear Mum and Dad, I think I know what's happened to Is. I've gone to see. Won't be long. See you tomorrow. Rob.'

And I put it on the kitchen worktop where I knew Mum would be sure to see it when she got home.

* * *

It was only when I was halfway into town that I realised how stupid I was; I hardly had any money and hadn't the vaguest idea how I was going to get to Wiltshire. All I had in my pockets was a scrunched-up pound note (this was long before we had pound coins) and a handful of coppers, plus the usual things boys of my age had, like elastic bands, sweet wrappers and lots of fluff.

By now I was in the High Street, passing the newsagents, greengrocers, butchers – the usual row of shops – when I saw a bus coming towards me. 'Slough' it said on its destination board. On impulse I ran to the bus stop, jumped on, and went upstairs. It was empty so I made my way right to the front, sitting above where the driver was. I threw my sleeping bag and duffle bag down on the seat beside me and made myself comfortable. It was obviously a really old bus. Several of the seats were torn and the ceiling, which had originally been bright white, was now stained nicotine yellow. But at least, and at last, I was on my way!

Slough I knew had a mainline railway station – and it was the mainline from London to Bristol – the very line Brunel had built! Surely it would take me straight to Box. But my enthusiasm quickly disappeared when I realised that the little money I had on me wasn't going to get me very far. By the time I'd paid my bus fare I had even less, but I decided to find out how much it would cost anyway.

'How much is a ticket to Box, please?' I asked the woman behind the glass panel in the station ticket office.

'Box?' she answered. 'Let me see,' and she ran her finger down a long list of station names. 'No Box here I'm afraid. Whereabouts is it?'

'It's in Wiltshire. There's a very famous tunnel there.'

'I dare say. But there's no station there, I'm afraid. Where's it close to?'

'I'm not sure... oh, yes, Bath I think. There's a station there, isn't there?'

'Bath Spa. Single or return?'

'Oh return... if I've got enough money.'

But as soon as she told me the price I realised that I didn't have enough.

'Oh, thanks,' I said and turned to go away.

'Don't you want a ticket then?' she called as I wandered back to the main station concourse. I stood around wondering what to do for a second and then the departure board over the entrance to the platforms caught my eye. There was, I saw, a train going to Bristol in five minutes, and it was bound to go through Bath. I walked up towards the platform.

In those days there were machines at the entrance to the platform where you could buy a 'platform ticket' for 1p, so you could meet someone from a train on the platform or wave them goodbye. Without thinking I dropped a coin in the machine, took my ticket and went on to the platform. A few minutes later, a distorted voice from the loud-speakers overhead announced the arrival of the train to Bristol Temple Meads and the voice had hardly finished when the train roared in.

Unlike the train that Is and I had travelled in up to London, this one was very new and very clean. I pulled open a door and got in, knowing that what I was doing was against the law. I had to find Is and that was all that mattered to me at the time. I had heard about people hiding in the toilets of trains to avoid the ticket inspector and that's what I thought I would do. I leaned out the open window and watched as the guard blew his whistle. The carriage I was in was quite close to the engine, so I figured it would be a while before he made his way up through the train. As the train pulled away I pulled my head back in and decided to settle down in a comfortable seat while keeping an eye out for him. The train picked up speed and I peered out of the window. The suburbs slid past as back gardens gradually gave way to more open countryside.

And then, without warning, the train was crossing a bridge and I looked down to see what was unmistakeably the Thames below. We were, I realised, on the Maidenhead bridge. The very bridge that Is had drawn in Mr Phillips' class and which he declared was 'impossible'. A grin spread across my face at the thought of her and how she had stood up to him; I closed my eyes and sighed.

'Tickets please!' said a voice only a few feet away and my eyes jerked open to see not the guard

I had seen before but someone else, another ticket inspector!

I panicked and began fumbling in my pockets, trying to look as if I was searching for my ticket.

'Ticket please,' he repeated a few inches from my face.

'Oh, I...' I started, 'I haven't got one.'

'Right,' he said, 'you're not allowed to travel without a ticket, you know that?'

'Yes, but... what I mean is that my dad has it and he's gone to the toilet.' I surprised myself by how easily the lie came to my lips. But I compounded it by saying 'he'll be back in a minute.'

'Right, I'll see him on the way back,' the ticket inspector said, apparently believing me, and he carried on his way saying, 'Tickets please.'

I breathed a sigh of relief but then panic set in again. Now what was I to do? If I hid in the toilet he would be sure to come looking for me, I thought. And I certainly didn't have enough money to pay the full fare.

It was amazing luck for me that the train began slowing down at that moment. It must have been stopping for signals, because the next scheduled station wasn't for ages. I grabbed my sleeping bag and other stuff and went into the corridor. Pulling a window down I stuck my head out to see where we were. The train was indeed stopping at some signals. Not only that but my carriage was coming into a small country station, certainly not one the train normally stopped at. It was my only chance. I leant out and turned the handle as the train came to a rest. In 1972 trains didn't have automatic door locks like they do now, so I was able to open the door and jump out. My feet had only just touched the platform when the train began moving again and I slammed the door shut.

As the train disappeared into the distance, I saw that the station I was at was not only small, but unstaffed. There was no one to stop me and ask for my ticket. I couldn't believe my good luck until I realised I was now stuck somewhere in the middle of nowhere with hardly any money and no means of getting out of there.

Still, at least the weather was mild, not raining like earlier, and it was still daylight. I walked along the platform until I came to a small wooden gate leading into a lane. There were so few houses it was difficult to see why it deserved a station at all. Ten minutes later, I was walking along a wider road but still one without, it seemed, any traffic. My idea, my only idea in fact, had been to try hitchhiking – something which was far more common years ago. But without cars it was a total non-starter so I plodded on. As I rounded a bend, however, I saw an encouraging sight, a roundabout. And there, on a road sign, were the magical words: 'The West'.

'Great!' I said out loud and positioned myself just after the roundabout facing what I fondly imagined would be the oncoming traffic. No such luck.

But after a while some cars and lorries did actually start heading down the road I was standing next to, and I stuck my thumb out, just like I'd seen people do when I'd been in a car with Mum and Dad. But nothing stopped for me. They just kept ploughing on into the distance.

'Pigs!' I yelled after them.

I'd been standing on the side of the road for nearly an hour and nothing looked like it was ever going to stop. I felt cold and hungry and was virtually on the point of getting the bus back home, when this old Morris Minor pulled in a little way in front of me.

Picking up my sleeping bag with one hand and slinging my duffle bag over my shoulder, I ran down the road, suddenly feeling warmer.

As I got alongside the car, the driver leant across and wound down the passenger window.

'Where you goin' to then?' came a gruff voice from inside.

'Bath. Or near it anyway.'

''Op in.'

I opened the door to the ancient Morris, which creaked and groaned alarmingly, and sat in the front seat cradling my grubby possessions.

'What you goin' there for then?' came the gruff voice again. And it was only then that I realised it was a she not a he speaking. Her hair was cut really short and she had on a baggy brown sweater and jeans. How was I supposed to tell the difference?

'Oh,' I said, startled momentarily by my discovery. 'Why am I going to Bath?'

'That's what I said, weren't it?'

'I'm going to meet a friend. Or hoping to,' I added.

'Right. That's all right then.'

After that we drove for miles without saying a word to each other and then suddenly the old Morris squeaked to a halt.

''Ere we are then.'

'Where?' I asked, puzzled.

'As far as I be going.'

'But where are we?' I asked with more than a hint of desperation in my voice.

'Where I do live. 'Op out, I be turnin' off 'ere.'

I didn't have much choice. Much as I couldn't abide the driver, it was with terrible reluctance that I left the warmth of the car. I had no sooner stepped on to the pavement than, with a rattle and a squeal, she trundled off up the road and turned into a side lane. The car didn't even have normal flashing indicators, I noticed. Instead it had a little orange arm that lit up as it came out of the side of the car.

'Great!' I muttered to myself and stamped my foot in anger. Unfortunately I happened to be standing right next to a puddle and water sprayed halfway up my leg.

By now thoroughly dispirited (as well as soaked), I tramped off, not knowing where I was – and, whatever road I was on, it obviously wasn't the main route to the west. There wasn't a car in sight.

After a while my feet started really aching. I couldn't have gone more than a couple of miles but it felt like ten. How I wish I had waited until Mum or Dad came back and told them my idea about where Is would be the next day.

I was almost on the point of crossing the road and walking back the other way when this car screamed to a halt.

'Where're you going?'

I hesitated before replying. The man asking the question wasn't even as friendly as the last driver and the question sounded more menacing.

'Box... near Bath...' I ventured, very unsure of myself.

'That's where we're going too,' came the reply. 'Get in.'

I did as I was told and straight away started getting worried. You hear about terrible things happening to kids that go off on their own. And I thought I was clever!

After all, the things in the newspapers could have happened to Is – might have happened to Is for all I knew. It was too horrible to think of. Here I was doing exactly the same thing, accepting a lift from these perfect strangers who were quite probably thieves or murderers or something.

There was a distinct smell of rubber as we shot off up the road. My head was thrown back into the seat and I grabbed hold of the door handle to steady myself.

How on earth they could be going to Box I didn't know. I could hardly find it on the map as it was.

'You did say you were – er – going to Box, didn't you?' I asked nervously, half hoping they'd say no and I could get out of this frantic, speed-limit-breaking nightmare journey.

'No, we said we were going to Bath. That do you?'

'Yes, thank you,' I said.

'You can thank us by keeping a sharp look out of the back window.'

'What for?'

'What you think – the fuzz.'

'The fuzz?'

'The police. Just keep your eyes peeled for anyone following us. Got that?'

'But why would anyone...' I started.

'There's been a drugs bust in town and we only just got out in time. That's all you need to know. The fuzz'll be looking for a car with two people in, not three, so you're a bit useful right now if you know what I mean.'

'Oh, right,' I said and swallowed. I didn't know whether to believe them or not. It was the stuff nightmares are made of. And I found myself longing for the comfort of my bedroom and the warmth of my own bed.

The thought of bed made me feel sleepy despite being hurled around in the back seat of this crazy swaying car. The movement started to make me feel sick and, tired as I was, I couldn't help closing my eyes.

'I said keep a sharp look out!' came a shout from the front seat and my eyelids flickered open again to face the angry eyes of the man driving the car. He was staring at me in the driving mirror.

Up till that point I hadn't really taken notice of the driver, who had been doing most of the talking.

But now I realised that he was what we used to call a hippy. He had long fair hair which trailed past his shoulders and got mixed up with the mass of fur on the collar of the suede Afghan coat he was wearing. His mate in the passenger seat had similar length brown hair. But at that point, turning round to talk, I saw it was not a man at all – but a woman. This journey was getting more confusing all the time.

'Don't worry about him,' she smiled. 'He's just feeling the stress. It's getting to him.'

She turned back to her companion and put her hand on his shoulder in a friendly way. 'Come on,' she said, 'let the kid sleep, we're far enough out of town now. You shouldn't be so paranoid.'

The driver's voice softened slightly as he glanced back at me. 'Oh, all right, have a kip if you need it.'

'Thank you,' I said, really too scared to say anything else. In truth I was too worried to sleep. For all I knew the car could be full of drugs and the police might suddenly appear at any time. I began clenching my hands tightly and realised I was sweating profusely. In desperation, to shut out the horror of what was happening, I closed my eyes...

When I opened them again all I could see were trees looming up in the headlights as we roared along a country road. I had obviously fallen asleep and now I had no idea where we were. All I knew was that it seemed I was trusting two probably very dangerous perfect strangers with my life.

And then suddenly, in a flash of light from the headlights, I saw the word 'Corsham' on a sign. And then, a bit further on, another sign. And, on it, there it was: 'Box'.

I couldn't believe it. I had made it seemingly in one piece.

'This is it!' I shouted.

'This is what?'

'Where I want to go.'

Miraculously, as I spoke, the car slowed down a bit and the crazy swaying I had experienced all the way ceased. We went through the town at a reasonable speed and the headlights picked out the cottages on either side. They were all stone and very old.

'Where d'you want dropping then?'

'Oh, anywhere here'll do,' I said, desperate to get away.

'Right.'

We went round a mini-roundabout and followed the road towards Bath. As we came out of the town and the road opened up, we pulled to a standstill.

'Here do?'

'Here will do fine,' I said, already pulling on the door handle to open it. 'Thanks a lot.'

The only answer I got was the sound of the car roaring off again into the distance, leaving me, my duffle bag and sleeping bag on the kerb, staring in surprise after it.

It took a few minutes for me to calm down and then I walked back into the village. There was nothing but cottages and once again I wished I was back in my warm bed. Then, to my great relief, I noticed what was obviously a railway bridge. The tunnel must be around here somewhere, I figured. I peered into the darkness but couldn't see anything as I followed the railway lines as far as my eyes would let me. Then I crossed over the road and peered in the other direction. There, only a few hundred yards away, was the dark outline of what was most definitely a tunnel. Without doubt.

Exhausted, weary, hugely relieved, but strangely satisfied, I set off to find somewhere to stay for the night. I decided to get off the main road as soon as possible and walked down a small side lane not knowing really where I was going. There were only streetlamps every now and again so it was really quite dark. I could hardly see a thing.

I walked on further, shivering a bit with the cold and thinking how ridiculous I was doing this at all. Then I came to what appeared to be a small farm and just beyond the gate was a barn. Perfect.

I slithered over the gate, keeping my two bags with me. The last thing I wanted was to drop either of them into what looked and felt like thick slimy mud. Or worse.

My feet made a squelchy noise as I tramped towards the barn. As I climbed up the bales of hay I realised how tired I was and how inviting the barn seemed. Sleep was all I craved. It was lucky I'd remembered to bring an alarm clock; I'd need that if I was going to wake up in time to get to the tunnel by dawn.

But as it turned out I needn't have worried. There was no way I was going to get any sleep that night at all.

I'd only just reached the top of the hay bales when a whole herd of cows started making its way towards the barn. Undaunted, I pulled aside some of the hay bales to make a hollow I could snuggle into, like a nest.

Early April isn't the best time to set off sleeping rough with only a sleeping bag, I can tell you. But at least the hay would keep the wind out, I thought. What it couldn't keep out was the noise.

The cows came closer and closer as I huddled myself into as small a ball as I could make. All the time they were mooing and sloshing around in the mud at the bottom of the hay barn.

Then they started pulling and munching at the hay on the lower bales. 'They'll eat their way to the top,' I thought to myself. 'Then they'll get me!' I no longer thought of them as a bunch of cows, more monsters, like something out of a horror movie.

But the worst thing, the very worst thing, was that they seemed to spend all night doing their business. There were the most disgusting plopping and splashing noises all around me. I looked at my watch: 12.30 a.m. Dawn, I reckoned, would be about 6.30 and that meant I needed to be away from the farm by, at the latest, 6.00 a.m. I seriously doubted there was any chance of sleep at all.

Then I started worrying about my chances of getting down from the hay loft in the morning – of ever getting down from it again in fact. The cows certainly showed no intention of moving. They just carried on munching and mooing and plopping and splashing. It was really more than I could bear.

Those next few hours were sheer hell. I couldn't do anything but lie there. I couldn't sleep. There was nothing I could do. I finished the last of my Swiss roll and waited. Then I wanted to go to the toilet myself. That was the worst thing of all. I couldn't do it here and there was no way I was going to push past those cows in the dark. I just hung on. It was torture.

But then, just when I was feeling I would burst, the cows suddenly moved away. With mournful moos they upped and went, without any warning. I could hear them trampling through the mud somewhere over the other side of the farm. It was such a relief.

I might have been relieved in one way, but not in the other. I scrambled down the bales as fast as I could and found a hidden corner behind the barn.

I looked at my watch again.

Five past six. Time to get to the tunnel.

12
Towards the Light

I shivered slightly in the early morning chill as I made my way up the lane back to the main road. When I got to the bridge I looked over and could see the vague shape of the tunnel mouth a few hundred yards in the distance.

The sky was an odd pale-grey colour and the trees showed as shadows against it. It was a strange sensation being up that time in the morning. I couldn't remember the last time I'd been up this early.

There was no sign of Is, but then I couldn't have expected to see her in that early morning light even if she had been there. I decided to go right down to the railway tracks themselves even though I knew that was against the law and very dangerous.

I crossed the road and got to a gate. It was

locked with a big padlock on it and barbed wire on the top. The fence on either side of the gate was also barbed wire, but on one side the middle wire had sagged, leaving a gap large enough to scramble through.

I was very nearly clear before I managed to snag my coat. There was a horrible ripping noise and I could just imagine what Mum was going to say when she saw what I'd done.

On the other side of the fence there were some steps which led down to a ramp underneath the road bridge.

The sky was lightening by the minute and was now a very very pale bluish colour. The tunnel was more distinct and I could see the grass banks on either side, and the shapes of other trees in the distance. Birds were singing now, welcoming the dawn.

Carefully I went down the last few steps, right down to the side of the track itself.

Is wasn't here at all, that much was clear. I had been wrong. It was nearly dawn proper by now. I didn't feel quite so cold by this time; I'd probably adjusted to the shock of being up so early.

It was very strange, watching the tunnel mouth become lighter and lighter as the day began. I think I'd expected dawn to happen all of a sudden somehow but here it was, just creeping up on me.

There was no sign of the sun either. Is's story about the tunnel was obviously just a myth. It had to be.

But where was she? Where on earth could she be? I had felt so sure that this was where she'd have come. After all, it was Brunel's birthday.

I stood still and listened for the slightest movement. Nothing. Only the chirping of birds and a light breeze blowing in the trees.

Every now and then a car went over the bridge I was standing underneath, someone on the way to work probably. I felt such a fool. I'd left home without telling my parents where I was going and by now they'd be as worried about me as everyone had been about Isabel.

I'd hitched all the way down here to stand in the cold, staring at a tunnel in the middle of the countryside for no reason at all. Now I was going to have to try to get lifts all the way back home again and face my parents' anger. All for nothing.

It was really quite light now. I could see the hillside on the other side of the tracks clearly, and even the fence that ran along the top. I hadn't noticed that before. The tunnel mouth itself has a sort of balustrade along the top too: really quite ornate.

I decided to walk right up to the tunnel to make

quite sure that Is wasn't around somewhere, hidden in the shadows behind a bush or tree.

Surprisingly, there was really very little room between the tracks themselves and the steep banks which rose up on either side. I was careful to stay as far away from the rails as I possibly could.

I crept towards the tunnel mouth, looking around me as I went. No, nothing. It was practically dawn. The sky was really very light and even though I couldn't see the sun there was certainly no sign of anything unusual coming through the tunnel.

I felt thoroughly miserable. I had had it with Is. I kicked a piece of ballast and went to turn round, to make my way home.

And, just as I did, a tiny speck of light appeared down in the depths of the tunnel, in the blackness.

I stared, amazed, as first one beam then another joined it and grew in size. There was now what looked like a small pinpoint of light suspended way, way in the distance.

It was a small, cold, yellowy light at first. But in no time at all, it grew more and more intense.

It was happening, it really was happening! Just as Is said it would!

The sun was rising through the great tunnel at Box!

There were now shafts of brilliant white light and in them I caught sight of something else. A black speck, as if I'd held up my thumb to the light. I couldn't make it out.

The speck moved. And it dawned on me what it was. It was Is, standing with her back to me, there in the middle of the tracks, some way down inside the tunnel.

I couldn't believe it. What was she doing? She was mad.

'Is! Is!' I yelled.

I could see her clearly outlined now as the sun burst through the tunnel.

'Is!' I screamed. 'Come back out here. What on earth are you doing in there? You'll be killed!'

She turned to look at me, and her face seemed pale and completely expressionless. It was as if she hadn't seen me at all. There was no recognition in her face. She had simply turned in the direction of my voice.

Is didn't say a word and then, unbelievably, she started walking away from me.

I hadn't seen a train all the time I'd been here, but there was bound to be one soon. This was complete, absolute madness.

'Is! Come back!' I yelled again, screaming at her. 'Is! Is!'

She walked away slowly into the tunnel, towards the light, towards the sun.

There was only one thing for it: I tore into the tunnel. Part way towards her I tripped on a sleeper and fell headfirst on to the track.

I looked up and she was still just walking slowly away as if she hadn't even noticed.

I got up and rushed after her again.

'For God's sake, Is! Come back!' My voice was choking and there was a stinging in my eyes. I knew I was about to start crying so I bit my lip. I felt terrified. It was only blind panic that pushed me on.

Is continued to ignore me as I pounded along the track.

Just as I reached her the sun disappeared. It had gone above the tunnel mouth at the other end to rise into the sky.

Inside the tunnel it was black again. But I was close enough to make her out.

Catching hold of her sleeve, I spun her around.

'Go away, leave me alone!' she cried.

'Is, come out of here! You'll be killed, we'll both be killed!'

She threw her head back defiantly. 'I don't care. I don't care.'

'You – are – coming – with – me,' I said, trying

hard to control my anger at her stupid behaviour.

For such a small girl she was surprisingly strong. I had to drag her back along the tunnel by the arm.

I pulled her towards the pale outline shape of the tunnel mouth we had come from.

'Come on, you're coming with me,' I said firmly.

After a while she resisted less and less. But when we were nearly back to the tunnel mouth, she turned around again.

'Oh, look!' she said in a far off sort of voice. 'The sun. It's come back!'

I turned to see what on earth she meant. There was a light, getting bigger again but not in the same way the sun had.

'It's a train!' I yelled. 'It's the light on the front of a train! It's the headlight. For God's sake, run!'

I pulled, dragged Is towards the safety of the circle of daylight in front of us.

This time, as we emerged from the tunnel, it was Is who tripped. She fell headlong right in the middle of the tracks.

I pulled her to her feet, her knee was bleeding but we managed to hobble over the tracks and threw ourselves on to the grass bank.

A second later, with a tremendous roar, the train came bursting out into the day. Lights from its windows went flashing past us as we lay there petrified just inches from the deadly steel wheels, slicing along the rails with a terrifying screeching sound.

As quickly as it appeared, it vanished. It had all happened so fast neither of us could believe it. Seeing a train go past that quickly and that close left us both terrified out of our wits.

We were both shaking and it wasn't from the cold.

Minutes passed before either of us said anything. We stared ahead looking at nothing. There was not a whisper of the train now. It had long gone. The only sound was the chirping of birds, as before.

Finally I forced myself to speak. 'You okay?'

Is turned her face towards me. There were tears streaming down, drawing patterns in the dirt on her cheeks.

'Yes – I think so,' she replied through sniffs.

'We could have been – killed.'

'I know.'

'But why? Why did you do it?'

'Don't ask.'

'That's what you always say.' I felt myself getting infuriated with her again. She'd nearly got us both killed and there wasn't as much as a word of thanks from her.

I sat looking at her, wondering what was going

170

on in that brain of hers. She did look a sight.

Her face was filthy and her hair was all straggly, strands of it stuck to her face with dirt and tears, her coat was ripped (as mine was, I remembered) and her knee looked a right mess.

'Your knee's still bleeding.'

'What?' She looked down at her bruised and scraped leg. 'Oh, yes.'

'Here.' I produced a handkerchief from my pocket. What I was doing with what was apparently a clean handkerchief I shall never know. I never usually carried one at all, let alone a clean one.

I tied it around her knee as best I could.

'There.'

'Thanks.' At last she thanked me, wonders would never cease.

'Are you going to tell me what all this is about then?'

'What what's about?'

'You know, why you ran away?'

'I would have thought that was obvious.'

'No. Just because of that bust up with Mr Phillips, you mean?'

'It was more than that. I felt I was becoming some sort of, I don't know, some sort of freak. Do you know what I mean?'

'You were going on a bit,' I admitted.

'How'd you find me then?'

'Easy!' I managed a small laugh. 'It's Brunel's birthday isn't it. When I thought about it, I knew this was the only place you could possibly be.'

'I didn't think you'd remember.' She looked in a distracted way towards the tunnel. 'I had to be here. I had to. He was a genius, wasn't he?'

'Isambard?'

'Who else?'

'And you still think you're – him?'

'I'm not so sure now.'

'Well, that's a relief.'

'When I was in that tunnel, walking towards the sun there, I felt I was Isambard stronger than I ever had before. Even stronger than when we had that stupid lesson with Mr Phillips about ships.'

'He was worried too, you know.'

'Who was? Mr Phillips? You've got to be joking!'

'No really, he was quite upset. I think he blamed himself for you disappearing.'

'Serve him right.'

'Oh come on. Anyway, I'm glad you're feeling better.'

I'd done it again. I'd gone and said something really stupid without thinking. Isabel glared at me, shooting daggers from the depths of her dark eyes.

'Feeling better? What do you mean "feeling

better"? I haven't been ill I'll have you know, Robert Morgan! Do you hear me?'

'You know what I mean...'

'No, I don't know what you mean. You think I'm mad, don't you, that's what you think.'

'Don't be daft.'

'"Don't be daft",' she mimicked me. 'I am not mad as it happens, despite what you might think. You may not believe in reincarnation and things like that, but it happens. People's spirits carry on. I was Isambard Kingdom Brunel in a previous life. I know it.'

'You said you weren't so sure a few minutes ago.'

'I KNOW IT!' She screamed at me so hard that spit covered my face. 'I am Isabel Williams only in body. I really am Isambard Brunel.'

She stood up awkwardly. Then, standing with her injured leg held out stiffly in front of her, she shouted out at the very top of her voice for all the world to hear:

'I AM ISAMBARD KINGDOM BRUNEL!'

I looked up at her, feeling rather scared. Then over her shoulder I saw something else. On the top of the road bridge, leaning over the parapet, a dozen or more people had gathered.

Not only that, but, making their way along

from the bridge down the side of the tracks were a policeman and a policewoman.

We didn't have to bother with hitching lifts back home. We had a ride in a police car. Someone had noticed us down there by the tunnel mouth and called the police.

By the time we got back home, everyone knew what had happened. There was quite a reception committee waiting for us at the police station. Mum and Dad were there, and Mrs Williams. A reporter from the local paper and loads of others. They all kept asking us questions all the time. Is sat there, stony faced, and said nothing. All I wanted to do was sleep. And, without warning, that's exactly what I did there and then, in the police station: fell asleep.

* * *

When I finally woke it was like I'd had a bad dream. I was back home in my bed. I rubbed my eyes and sat up. It was late Sunday afternoon. My mum came in with a cup of tea as soon as she heard me stir.

'Here you are,' she said and sat on the edge of my bed with a smile.

'How's Is?' was the first thing I said.

'Oh, she's fine, I think. None the worse for

wear. How about you?'

'Okay.'

'Good.'

'Mum...'

'Yes, Rob?'

'I'm sorry.'

'We won't say another word about it. I'm just glad you're safe and sound. And glad Isabel is as well.'

'Can I go and see her. I'd like that.'

'I expect so. Tomorrow. But just you rest for a bit first, eh?'

But when tomorrow came I didn't see Is. And, to be honest, I don't think I had really expected to.

Mr Gregory swept into the class in his usual bull-like fashion and started going through the register. But, when he got to Williams, he stopped.

'Isabel Williams, I have to tell you,' he said solemnly, 'will not be returning to us at St Leonards School. Her mother has wisely decided to take her to another school. In Devon, I understand, where she has relatives.'

And that was that.

* * *

All this happened more than thirty years ago.

A lot can happen in that time. Is's mum sold the house in Walton Road a few months after they moved to Devon. Originally they had gone to stay with Is's Aunt Kate – her dad's sister (I didn't even know she had an aunt) who lived in Plymouth. But, when the house was sold, her mum bought a little cottage on the edge of Dartmoor.

Is wrote to me to tell me all about it. It was quite small, she said, with tiny windows and a little winding staircase – but quite lovely and built from local granite. 'It's been here for centuries and I doubt it'll ever fall down,' she wrote, 'it's as if it were carved right out of the hillside itself.' It was no surprise that she went on to say that Ashburton itself used to be at the end of a Great Western Railway branch line, built of course to Brunel's 7-foot wide broad gauge. A preservation society was apparently running steam trains along some of the old line, so no doubt she was happy about that.

She also said she'd been to see what she described as 'Brunel's last and greatest bridge, completed the year he died': the Royal Albert Bridge across the River Tamar, separating Devon from Cornwall. I must say I was pleased to hear her talking about Brunel as another person and not herself. Perhaps she was finally accepting that she was Isabel Williams, plain and simple.

We exchanged quite a few letters and she sent me some photographs once, including some of the small terrier dog she called 'Brandy', which she used to take out on the moors. I kept her up to date with what was happening at school, especially the great news that old Phillips had got sacked for losing his temper good and proper one day and hitting one of the boys in the first year really hard. Serve him right – Phillips, that is, not the boy.

But then, in the way these things do, the letters became fewer and eventually stopped. The last I heard she was going to move again but she didn't say where. 'Going West' was all she said.

I haven't kept in touch with anyone else much from Class 2F. Although I did get invited to Veronica Biggleswade's wedding a good few years ago, but I couldn't go – I can't remember why. And I bet even as you read this, someone, somewhere is being bored stupid by Clever Trevor.

One incredible bit of news I did pick up was that Kevin Ryder actually managed to become famous (for all of a week). He formed a band called the 'Electric Shavers' some time in the 80s, which was a sort of post-punk band, a bit like the Psychedelic Furs so people said. Since I had no idea who the Psychedelic Furs were that wasn't a very useful comparison. But (difficult to believe, I know) the Electric Shavers had a record that actually scraped into the top forty.

I never got any money back on my investment though.

I ended up working as a journalist for a local newspaper and then for various magazines in London. And it was while working for one of them that I found myself having to do some research about Brunel for an article I was writing. I spent some time in the Science Museum, which I hadn't been to since that day when Is first showed me the model of the Great Eastern. It was still where we'd left it, in its glass case. The Caerphilly Castle, the steam engine where Kevin Ryder had accused Is and me of having 'a little cuddle by the choo-choos', wasn't there any longer, though. It was moved in 1999 to the Great Western Railway Museum in Swindon, where it still is as far as I know.

I also spent a few hours in the Brunel Museum in Rotherhithe, which is at the other end of the tunnel under the Thames where Is first announced to me her conviction that she was Isambard Brunel reincarnated. It was there I first heard about Brunel's older sister Sophia. She, it seems, was extremely talented – able to discuss engineering matters with her brother and father with complete authority. In fact, her knowledge of engineering was so good that she was described by Lord Armstrong (another famous Victorian engineer) as 'Brunel in Petticoats'. I wonder if Is ever knew that. It would make her smile, I bet. Sophia went on to marry Benjamin Hawes, who became a government minister and Sir Benjamin Hawes – so she became Lady Hawes. In Victorian times, of course, there was no chance of her becoming an engineer like her father and brother even if she had wanted to.

Finally, about three years ago, having got fed up with the rat race, I and my family moved to West Wales. We moved to Pembrokeshire away from all the hustle and bustle of London. As it turned out, though, I didn't get away from Brunel. Where we moved to was a few miles from a place called Neyland, a small town with a few shops and a marina on the banks of Milford Haven. A hundred and fifty years ago it was where Brunel decided to site the far western terminus of his Great Western Railway.

Despite having lived in Pembrokeshire for three years, I hadn't actually been to Neyland until about six months ago. There's hardly anything left of what was a major railway terminus now; just a few lengths of railway line buried in tarmac. But there are some railings actually made from Brunel's original broad-gauge track, which must be very rare. From Neyland, packet steamers and other boats would go to Ireland and beyond. The water in Milford Haven is incredibly deep and so the largest ships can come in and out easily. Today huge oil tankers use the haven all the time. And I wasn't surprised to find out that Brunel's monster ship the Great Eastern twice came into Neyland for repairs.

The Great Eastern! I can remember the day Is stormed out of Mr Phillips' class as if it were yesterday. That great ship – a ship that was really too big, too ahead of her time – only managed to make money laying the first telephone cables across the Atlantic. She was the only ship large enough to carry the 3000 miles of cable needed to reach America.

Another connection with America was made that day I went to Neyland. To be honest I'm not even sure why I went, but I parked the car and walked along the quay where the station would have been. I'd bought a sandwich and newspaper and I sat on a bench overlooking the haven, watching some yachts sail up and down. I opened my packet of sandwiches and took a bite while enjoying the sun and light breeze on my face. Then I opened the newspaper... and couldn't believe my eyes. Staring back at me was Is! It was definitely her. I hadn't seen her for more than 30 years, but it was unmistakably her. I was so astonished at seeing her photograph that it took me a couple of minutes to realise why it was there. Underneath the picture the headline read: 'British Engineer in First Manned Mission to Mars'.

My hands were shaking with excitement as I continued reading. 'One of the teams working on the project,' the article said 'is led by a woman engineer from Britain called Isabel Williams.' Not only a British engineer; not only a woman engineer that it was true, I read it out loud: 'NASA describes Isabel Williams as an extremely talented engineer whose contribution is invaluable to the project. She has the flair and imagination to think the unthinkable, to think big and to make things happen.'

'Of course she does!' I yelled. 'Of course she does!'

Realising I was shouting out loud, I turned around nervously to see if anyone had heard me. And my eyes were drawn across the grass to a statue on the other side of the road. There, in bronze, with his trademark top hat – clutching a ship in one hand and a railway engine in the other – was a statue of Brunel. I left my sandwich on the bench and ran over the road.

I was still holding the newspaper as I looked up at Brunel and suddenly I felt the hairs on the back of my neck stand up. There was something about the set of the jaw line, the proudness of the lips and the way the eyes looked that seemed so very, very familiar.

I looked at the photograph of Is in the paper. I looked back at the statue. I felt tears well up in my eyes.

'Is, you did it!' I cried, 'You did it!'

I stood looking up at that statue for ages. People probably thought I was barmy.

Isambard Kingdom Brunel was probably the greatest engineer of his time, some say the greatest engineer ever. He was born at the beginning of the nineteenth century and in his lifetime he was responsible for the Great Western Railway and twenty-five other railways, more than 100 bridges, eight dock systems, three ships and a pre-fabricated hospital.

Everything he did had to be bigger, better, longer, faster. He worked on the first tunnel ever built underwater. He built the longest tunnel and the fastest train. Each of the three ships he built was the largest the world had ever seen when launched. He was only five feet tall – but in engineering terms Brunel was a giant.

Derek Webb was brought up in Portsmouth (where Brunel was born) and now lives in Pembrokeshire with his wife and son. He spent many years working as a creative director in a variety of major advertising agencies, before becoming a freelance scriptwriter and director in 1996. He is also a successful playwright with a number of stage plays published and professionally produced. His work for children includes dramatising a large number of books for audio, including *The Minpins* and *Esio Trot* by Roald Dahl; several of Enid Blyton's *Famous Five* and *Secret Seven* stories; and eighty minute dramatisations of children's classics including *The Secret Garden*, *The Railway Children* and *The Incredible Journey*. He has also written a number of short stories for younger readers called *Popplejoy and.... Is* is his first full-length children's novel.

Find out more about Is and Brunel at

www.ikbrunel.org.uk